ANGEL
IN
HEAVY
SHOES

ANGEL IN HEAVY SHOES

A Katie Rose Story

Lenora Mattingly Weber

Thomas Y. Crowell Company   New York

Designed by SALLIE BALDWIN KASELER

PUBLISHED IN CANADA BY
FITZHENRY & WHITESIDE LIMITED, TORONTO

L.C. Card 68-13589

ISBN 0-690-09189-3

3   4   5   6   7   8   9   10

BY LENORA MATTINGLY WEBER

MY TRUE LOVE WAITS

MEET THE MALONES

BEANY MALONE

LEAVE IT TO BEANY!

BEANY AND THE BECKONING ROAD

BEANY HAS A SECRET LIFE

MAKE A WISH FOR ME: A BEANY MALONE STORY

HAPPY BIRTHDAY, DEAR BEANY

THE MORE THE MERRIER: A BEANY MALONE STORY

A BRIGHT STAR FALLS: A BEANY MALONE STORY

WELCOME, STRANGER: A BEANY MALONE STORY

PICK A NEW DREAM: A BEANY MALONE STORY

TARRY AWHILE: A BEANY MALONE STORY

SOMETHING BORROWED, SOMETHING BLUE: A BEANY
  MALONE STORY

COME BACK, WHEREVER YOU ARE: A BEANY MALONE STORY

THE BEANY MALONE COOKBOOK

DON'T CALL ME KATIE ROSE

THE WINDS OF MARCH: A KATIE ROSE STORY

A NEW AND DIFFERENT SUMMER: A KATIE ROSE STORY

I MET A BOY I USED TO KNOW: A KATIE ROSE STORY

ANGEL IN HEAVY SHOES: A KATIE ROSE STORY

HOW LONG IS ALWAYS? A STACY BELFORD STORY

HELLO, MY LOVE, GOOD-BYE: A STACY BELFORD STORY

SOMETIMES A STRANGER: A STACY BELFORD STORY

TO CAROL,
the youngest Mrs. Weber

CONTENTS

ANGEL
IN
HEAVY
SHOES

PART ONE

Wednesday

❧ 1 ❧

It always took Katie Rose longer to dress for school than it did her younger sister Stacy who shared the same room and double bed with her. (Katie Rose's small and worshipful blond poodle made a third inmate of the room and bed. He was supposed to sleep at the foot of the bed outside the covers, but many chill mornings he was found at the head of the bed and under the covers.)

But then the reason Stacy could make good time at dressing was because she wore a uniform and therefore had no *decisions* to slow her.

On this Wednesday morning in mid-October, Stacy donned her white blouse, pleated plaid skirt, and kelly green blazer with the intertwined initials,

SJH for St. Jude's High, on the pocket. She whisked a comb through her shoulder-length auburn-blond hair and transformed it into a wavy pony tail by tying a somewhat bedraggled green ribbon around it. She was ready to go bouncing down the stairs before Katie Rose decided, because of the bright and warm sun, to shuck off her purple slipover, and replace it with a sleeveless blouse.

Stacy said over her shoulder from the top of the stairs, "I forgot to put up lunches last night. I'll bet I catch Holy Ned from Ben."

Ben was the oldest of the six Belford children.

Katie Rose smoothed her short, black hair that had been mussed by pulling off the slipover. Any minute now Ben would call up the stairs, "We could do with less primping and more help around here in the morning." She held her comb poised with the almost sobering realization that Ben hadn't yelled that up the stairs for—oh, it must have been several weeks.

She started down the stairs just as Stacy came bounding back up. She held out her hand with a fringe of broom straws between her thumb and index finger and said, all in one breath, "I had to give you peanut butter so don't forget to stop after school and get lunch meat—oh yes, and sandwich bread at Pearl's Bakery—and there are only three peaches, so draw a straw to see whether you get one or a little shrinkled apple."

No one could misuse, mispronounce, or coin new words so readily as Stacy. It seemed to Katie Rose that she went through life correcting her. It didn't bother Stacy who had more bounce to the ounce than anyone Katie Rose knew. She answered Katie Rose's "Not *shrinkled*. Either shriveled or wrinkled," with, "You'll think it's shrinkled when you eat it at lunch. You got a short straw."

"Did you catch it from Ben for not fixing the lunches last night?"

"Sh-h-h! He hasn't even noticed."

In the kitchen, Katie Rose turned a puzzled look on Ben, who wasn't giving Stacy Holy Ned for adding to the breakfast hubbub by lunch making. He hadn't even noticed how long she, Katie Rose, took to dress because he didn't say in his veddy-veddy voice, "The Dutchess of Belford descends from her boudoir." (Bude-wah, he pronounced it.)

He was at the stove where oatmeal was cooking, and where a percolator burbled and gave out the brown smell of coffee. He was tall, with no flesh to spare on his big bones. His thin face with its squarish chin was still reddened from his summer's work on a road-building crew. His skin didn't take a bronze tan; it burned, and then peeled, and then burned again. His hair was a shade redder than Stacy's, and his eyes were as blue as eyes could be.

From the time of their father's death four years before, Mother had leaned heavily on Ben. She was loving, impulsive, and so short-tempered that she was swift to reach out to clout an offender. But she was no disciplinarian. Ben was. Mother had no head

5

for figures. Ben had. "Old crack-the-whip Ben," Katie Rose often sputtered with the resentment of a sister who was only a year and a half younger than he.

She had certainly never thought she would miss or be vaguely troubled by Ben who was so lost in his own thoughts that he failed to crack the whip. Something else was missing too. He always timed the cooking of the oatmeal to his singing "Rose of Tralee." Katie Rose had never realized until this Indian summer morning in October that his strong, rich tenor filling the whole lower floor was a nice way to start the day.

The three younger Belfords were setting the table in the dinette that adjoined the kitchen. Katie Rose dropped bread in the toaster and said, "For heaven's sake. Can't you three put down a plate without thumping it down? Can't you put on silver without banging it?"

Three pairs of reproachful slate-blue eyes were turned toward her. Their audible mutter was, "We gotta hurry so's to feed our mice and our turtle," and the near inaudible one which she wasn't meant to hear was, "Katie-Rose-go-blow-your-nose."

The three youngest Belfords, who attended St. Jude's grammar school, were always lumped together for convenience sake as the littles. They were all of a size, although Matt and Jill were twins and Brian was a year younger. Brian had an inherent gentleness and courtesy which seldom showed because he felt he had to keep up with the tough and rowdy twins. Ben always said that Jill didn't know yet she wasn't a boy. Katie Rose suspected that she was beginning to know, but that she wasn't ready yet to give up the rough and tumble life she shared with her brothers. She was the spokesman for the three.

Mother came into the kitchen and stopped close to the stove and the percolating coffee. She was the kind who gave a lift to any room she walked into, even though, as on this morning, her sleepy face was still damp from the cold water she had sloshed over it and she clutched a faded robe over her gown. She half yawned, half spoke, "Isn't the coffee ready yet?" She always said that she was a walking zombie in the morning until she had a cup of coffee. For her job was playing the piano and singing requests at a supper club every night except Friday and Sunday. The supper club, called Guido's Gay Nineties, was five miles out on the Henderson Road. Her hours were supposedly from eight to midnight, but it was usually closer to two when she returned.

It was always easy for the young Belfords to figure out their mother's age. She had been twenty when Ben was born and he, a sophomore at the university, was nineteen. She had been Rose O'Byrne before she married, and she had the O'Byrne red hair and the glowing transparent skin that went with it. Add to that sparkling blue eyes, a spontaneous laugh, no spread in her waistline, and it was little wonder Katie Rose was always hearing, "I can't believe your mother has six children, and one in college. She looks so young and pretty."

And what was more, Katie Rose realized, Mother, like Stacy, never worked at or worried about being pretty.

The noise and tempo in the kitchen increased. Stacy's knife squeaked as she scraped the bottom of the peanut butter jar. Ben broke eggs into the skillet. Cully, their big, overly friendly, overly hungry dog was everywhere underfoot, hoping that something would be spilled or dropped. The littles were now filling two very scummy looking saucers, one with water and one with raw oatmeal. This was the daily food and drink for the white mice, Gertie and George, who inhabited a copper cage in their room. Katie Rose wondered if they had ever once carried up those saucers without slopping over the contents on the stairs.

Upon returning, Brian gave them all his guileless smile. "I think they're getting tired of oatmeal."

"Are they, darlin' dear?" Mother said vaguely.

"Too darn' bad about them," Ben said shortly.

Stacy was popping open each paper sack with a bang before filling it with lunch. "Not so loud, child," Mother said, and added in her same vague and sleepy fashion, "I thought you fixed the lunches at night."

Stacy glanced uneasily at Ben. "Sometimes I do, but they're really more paleatable if I fix them just before we leave."

Sleepy or wide-awake Mother's laugh was always ready to spill over. It did now as Katie Rose said automatically, "You mean pal'-atable."

"Seems like it ought to be pal-*eat'*-able," Stacy insisted.

Ben said, "Hand down the bowls for the oatmeal, Katie Rose."

She held them out for his generous helpings. "Don't give me so much."

"You need to eat a good breakfast." But he said it tonelessly, as though some discomfort inside him was so great that all else lost importance.

It was when they were all at the breakfast table that Katie Rose spilled the salt. Mother's eyes opened wide, and she cried out, "Something unexpected is going to happen. Quick, lovey, throw some over your left shoulder to take the evil out of whatever it is."

The salt wasn't in a shaker but in a small glass saltcellar shaped like a gondola. Mother had bought it and its top-heavy spoon at one of the church rummage sales from which she always returned happily laden.

Katie Rose lost no time in picking up a pinch of the spilled salt and tossing it over her left shoulder. And then one of those crazy, unbelievable things happened. Stacy reached out to right the gondola, and *she* spilled it. She let out an *eeck!*—and hastily sprayed salt over her shoulder. Ben, with a muttered, "Oh, for Pete's sake!" straightened the cellar onto its narrow bottom, but just as he stuck the spoon back, it overbalanced and tipped over again.

"More and more unexpecteds," exulted one of the twins.

"Ben, throw some over *your* shoulder," Mother warned.

"Don't be silly. That's a lot of superstitious poppycock."

"I suppose it is," she admitted, "but I always feel better if I do."

"Will it be a nice unexpected?" Jill asked, and Brian added with his seraphic smile, "Maybe St. Jude's will burn to the ground."

Mother reached for him with an open palm, but her reach wasn't long enough. "Don't even say such a thing!" she scolded.

A whistle sounded outside, and the littles slid from the long bench. The four at the table winced each time one of them, following Ben's dictum, clattered his armful of dishes and silverware onto the sink board. The three muttered good-bys, and Brian took a moment to say gravely, "I guess I don't want St. Jude's to burn all the way down. Just maybe a kinda little fire."

Three bicycles were pulled away from their leaning positions at the back of the dinette—and then all was quiet. "I can't believe it," Mother said, and reached for a cigarette. "No one broke a bowl or glass. No one forgot his lunch, and none of the bikes had a flat tire."

Stacy said, "Are you sure, Mom, that if you throw

salt over your left shoulder it'll make the something unexpected a nice something?"

"Go on with you," Mother evaded. "I'm not sure of anything, and the older I get the un-surer I get."

No one answered. Each one sat in a gray study.

Katie Rose's pulse beat faster. *I'm starting my senior year at John Quincy Adams. I don't want to be a nonentity. I don't want to be just one of the hundred and forty-seven graduates. Ben says I have a duchess complex, but I can't help it. I want to be the kind to be pointed out, "There's Katie Rose Belford. She's the girl who—" If only the unexpected would fill in the blank after the "who—"*

Something unexpected, Stacy thought in wistful longing. *The nicest unexpected that could happen would be for Bruce and me to be the way we used to be. We didn't used to be so picky and fault-finding and just plain nasty-mean to each other. Maybe the unexpected will happen, and it'll change back to being as delightsome as it was when we first knew each other.*

Ben was minutely scraping up the film of salt on the table mat. *Mom, and her crazy superstitions!* But in spite of his scoffing, a tormented prayer rose in his throat: *Let the unexpected happen today. Let me be free of Holly and her dark spell. Let me laugh her off so I can be myself and go my own way again.*

11

Although Ben was usually the one who watched the clock to see that everyone got to where he had to be on time, this morning it was Mother who said, "Look at the time, Ben."

Stacy rushed through the house to gather up her books. In the old Belford Chevy with its cracked window, Ben would drive her to St. Jude's and then go on to the university.

Now only Katie Rose and Mother were left at the dinette table. Mother poured herself another cup of coffee, taking a wary sip to see how hot it was. "What do you suppose is eating Ben lately, Katie Rose?"

So Mother too had missed Ben's scolding and bossing and his "Rose of Tralee" while the oatmeal bubbled!

"Don't ask me, Mom."

"It isn't Jeanie, is it?"

"Not that I know of. We haven't had much chance to visit the last week or two because she's working early and late to get out the school paper."

Jeanie Kincaid was Katie Rose's best friend at Adams High. She and Ben had been dating for a year or two. It was Jeanie who always countered Katie Rose's exasperated "That old bossy Ben!" with a crinkly eyed smile and an "I like bossy men."

And Mother, who worried about how much they all leaned on Ben and grieved that he would be an old man before his time, always said, "Jeanie's good for him." It was true. The Ben who danced so expertly with Jeanie, whose hearty guffaw was like a gale that shook a room, who sang with such exuberance, "I dream of Jeanie with the cinnamon-brown hair," was not the same Ben who laid down the law to the littles, or worried about household bills.

Another sip of coffee and Mother mused, "Stacy's growing up. Goodness, sixteen. You know, lovey, I never quite trusted that starry-eyed ex-stacy, as she pronounces ecstasy, that she and Bruce had for each other. I had a hunch it couldn't last. They seem to be having rough going."

What queer turns life took! It was hard for Katie Rose, beginning her senior year, to believe that she'd gone through a time of yearning over the handsome star athlete at Adams High named Bruce Seerie. And a time when life had the taste of blackened bread because he showed preference for her ebullient, redheaded sister. Bruce and Stacy. Their romance certainly had had all the earmarks of "the world well lost for love" when it began.

Katie Rose said, "They're forever quarreling, and each time Stacy is sure they'll never be recon*cided,* as she puts it. That's the awful part of her mispronouncing words—we all say them without realizing it."

Mother laughed. "I know. She's got everyone calling Pikes Peak, Piker's Peak." And then more soberly, "I wish she and Bruce would be recon*cided* for good, or else break it off. His parents are so different." She groped for words, "You wouldn't think anyone could be *too* exemplary, or *too* worthy, or *too* law abiding. But they're so cussed righteous—he with his lawyering, and she with her Great Books and her Save Our Old Landmarks."

She added with disarming honesty, "That kind of a woman petrifies me. You can't imagine her ever having a run in her stocking, or being dunned by the phone company, or whacking a wet mop on a kid's bottom. Bruce and Stacy are so different too."

"Aren't opposites supposed to attract?"

"Yes, they attract. And then so often the very traits that attracted can irritate the other beyond endurance."

Cully's deep bark and the poodle's higher pitched one announced the arrival of the small blue Triumph and its driver, Miguel, who always called for Katie Rose. She too made a hurried dash for her armful of books. She called good-by to her mother, and bent down to pat and to explain, as she always did, to the unhappy little poodle, "Don't grieve, Sidewinder, I'll be back."

The boy who met her at the picket gate and took her books was tall and lanky with joints that seemed loosely put together. Under a thatch of straw-colored hair, his deep-set gray eyes were both thoughtful and roguish.

"Hi, Petunia. Did you say your morning prayers, brush your teeth, and put something extra in your lunch for me?"

"It was Stacy's turn to fix lunches. But I'm sure she put in an extra *shrinkled* apple for you."

He helped her over the car door which wouldn't

open, and put her books on the floor. He took off the camera he had strapped over his shoulder and laid it on her lap. "Coddle the Leica carefully," he said as he drove off. "I have to get another picture or two at school for the *Adams Advocate.*"

Miguel's real name was Michael Parnell, but he had come to Adams High from a school in Mexico, and the Miguel on his transcript had somehow stuck. His father, also named Michael, was a writer with six best sellers to his credit. He was now in Hawaii finishing a seventh book while Miguel stayed with his grandparents. He was often pointed out in Adams High halls as the boy who had traveled all over the world and could speak seven languages. That was a gross exaggeration, Miguel said; he could converse in three, and knew only enough in the others to say hello, good-by, I love you, where is, and how much.

Even so, Miguel was one of the pointed outs, along with the boy high-diving champion, the Negro girl who had rescued a child from a burning house, the pretty blond and latest Miss University Hills, and the Japanese girl who had won a prize for her rock garden, which had a pool with a bridge across it.

Jeanie too. "That's Jeanie Kincaid. She's the editor in chief of the paper."

"Who's that girl with her?"

"Just Jeanie's friend. Nobody in particular."

But this bright October morning, Katie Rose's voice was all lilt. "Guess what, Miguel? I spilled

the salt this morning, and that means that something unexpected is going to happen."

His grin was singular in that it conveyed his love
for life, the world, the people in it, and for the dark-
haired girl beside him. "In case we hit a truck, hang
on to the camera," he said.

2

Katie Rose and Jeanie walked out of seventh-hour psych which was their final class of the day.

Last year's yearbook had described Jeanie Kincaid as "a little girl with a lot of push, brains, and smile." The push and brains were responsible, no doubt, for her being editor in chief in her senior year of the *Adams Advocate*. The lot of smile was a crinkly one that almost closed her cinnamon-brown eyes. The cinnamon-brown hair, which Ben Belford sang of, sometimes looked too thick and heavy for a girl of five feet two, with a slim, elfin face.

Jeanie, an only child, envied Katie Rose the constant hubbub of her family, and several times had announced to their lunch table of eight, "If Ben

17

Belford ever asks me to marry him, I'll say yes, just so I'll have a Grandda and Gran O'Byrne and all that big family with their bear hugs and blarney."

Katie Rose had moments, such as when one of the littles' white mice escaped in the house, or when Ben called her the Duchess of Belford, or when Stacy left her washed and still wet sweater on their bed, when she envied Jeanie for being an only child and having a room of her own.

The two girls slowed their steps at the drinking fountain outside the auditorium where Miguel usually joined them. Katie Rose said, "I have to stop at the store on my way home. Are you too tied up to go along?" Jeanie was answering, "I'll say I'm tied up. There's that unwritten law that the first edition of the *Advocate* must see the light of day on the second Friday in October, which is day after tomorrow—" when Miguel came loping down the hall.

He skidded to a stop. "Has the unexpected that you've been expecting since you spilled the salt this morning happened yet, Petunia?"

"No, sir. Not an unexpected in a carload."

They started past the open door of the green room at the side of the auditorium stage. And then, by one of life's coincidences, Mrs. Dujardin, the drama teacher, called out, "Katie Rose, I was in hopes I'd see you. I've just had the most unexpected news. Come in, all of you."

Mrs. Dujardin, usually referred to behind her back as Mrs. Du, was a large, full-bosomed woman with striking black eyes and black hair which she swept back dramatically into more of a flange than a bun on top of her head. She was partial to black apparel and, on special occasions enhanced it with heavy, arty jewelry, and even a scarlet shawl with a wide fringe.

The three pushed into the small greenroom which to Katie Rose always had the delectable sight, sound, and smell of theater. Today, costumes were draped over chairs, and books of plays were spilled over Mrs. Dujardin's desk. Howard, president of the drama club for two years now, was at the typewriter. Christopher, a talented boy with unbelievably long and deft hands, was hunkered down on his heels, spraying silver paint on a pasteboard sword. The etherish smell of quick-drying paint vied with the coffee smell from the percolator Mrs. Dujardin always kept plugged in.

She said again, "Katie Rose, you're the very one we wanted to see. Christopher and Howard were just saying—"

Christopher flashed her his smile that did so much for his solemn face. "We said you were our best bet, Katie Rose."

"Your best bet!"

"I just had a phone call from Harriet Cass," the drama teacher explained. "And she's coming out tomorrow to tell the Drama Club and the Scribblers about a one-act play contest she's helping to sponsor."

Miguel gave a low whistle. "Harriet in the flesh! Imagine getting a good look at the playwright of *Grab Bag*."

Harriet Cass had written other plays. But *Grab Bag* had been a smash hit on Broadway, playing SRO for over a year. Katie Rose had seen it once on the stage and twice on the screen.

"Imagine getting a million smackeroos from the movies for it," Howard said over the pounding of his typewriter.

Katie Rose was incapable of saying anything.

Mrs. Dujardin went on, "This contest is Harriet Cass's pet. Of course, even a one-act takes so much time and hard work that I'm sure we can work out an arrangement for the English teachers to let it count toward your semester's work. I told Harriet about you, Katie Rose, and the skit you wrote for last Valentine's Day, and what good theater it was. She'd like to meet you when she comes tomorrow."

Katie Rose's hand went to her throat where a pulse was throbbing . . . *See that girl? That's Katie Rose Belford who wrote a play that won a prize.*

Howard tore his pages out of the typewriter, separated the two white sheets from the clinging carbon. "One for the bulletin board, and one for ye editor. I figured Harriet rated a splash in your paper, Jeanie."

"She rates a front-page splash." She wrinkled her nose as she always did when she was concentrating. Katie Rose read over her shoulder,

SPECIAL MEETING
Tomorrow, Thursday, October 12 at 3:15
Harriet Cass, Noted Playwright—

Jeanie was saying, "Miguel, we have to get our dummy to the printer's by five tomorrow. He might give us till five-thirty. Even that's clipping it pretty close."

"If Paul Revere made it, we can," he said.

Katie Rose walked out of the green room with them. Mrs. Dujardin had one final word, "You could even talk over your idea for a one-act with Harriet Cass tomorrow."

"I haven't an idea—not yet."

She said it again to Miguel and Jeanie as they stood for a minute at the head of the stairs before they went on to the journalism room, headquarters for the paper, "I haven't a ghost of an idea for a play."

Miguel gave her his fond, encouraging smile. "You'll come up with something, petty doll. Remember what Pop always says about a writer's subconscious."

"Tell me what he said again."

"He says every writer's subconscious is like a well-stocked deep freeze. So when he's in need of an idea or character or locale, all he has to do is reach in and pull one out."

"I've got a scrapbook of ideas I've scribbled down," she murmured.

The halls had quieted somewhat when she stood

21

at her open locker. Absentmindedly, she put on her sweater and piled books into her arms. Then she put them on the floor at her feet and extracted the scrapbook her lit teacher urged his students to keep. "Jot down anything that stirs or stimulates you. Let it be a hodgepodge. That's what the mind is."

She opened the notebook and her eyes rested on, "A proverb is but a halfway house to an idea." Well, if an idea would only come halfway, she'd go out and meet it. She smiled when reading the next quotation, "A star danced and under it I was born," because in her mind she always substituted Stacy for I. Stacy was the one who danced down the stairs each morning in a strike-up-the-band well-being.

On the next page she had written a brief summing up of Browning's *Pippa Passes* after reading it for lit: "The story of a naïve, optimistic factory girl, who has one day off from work and goes through it singing out her joy and goodness and trustfulness. Her chance appearances affect the spiritual life-histories of others as she passes."

Katie Rose murmured under her breath, "Pippa was pretty saccharine to believe, but still—"

She stood, holding her scrapbook, quite unconscious of two boys scuffling at the next tier of lockers or of the cessation when the hall monitor walked toward them. She didn't hear the muted notes of the orchestra practicing for the Halloween dance.

For she began to feel a certain stirring in her being, a certain receptive waiting for voices—

She was rudely roused by, "Hey, Katie Rose! You'll be going past the store on your way home, won't you?"

It took Katie Rose a dazed moment to focus on the speaker. She was a classmate with a sharp face under a bouffant hair-do which looked untidy after a school day. Rita Flood! Leave it to Rita to barge in just when a glimmer of an idea was beginning to tug at her elbow.

"Well, are you or aren't you going to stop at Wetzel's on your way home?" Rita demanded.

"Yes, I'm stopping there."

. . . Katie Rose had often grumbled to Jeanie Kincaid, "Honestly!—Rita Flood seems to think she has a lien on me just because we both went to St. Jude's grammar school. Ben is always calling me a snob but, I swear, even if Rita came from one of our first families, I still wouldn't like her. I feel sorry for her—"

Jeanie had put in readily, "You can feel sorry for a person without liking him or her." . . .

"I want you to tell Lennie something for me," Rita was saying. Lennie was her young brother who went to St. Jude's with the Belford littles.

"Why can't you tell Lennie yourself?"

"Well, you are behind the times, Katie Rose," Rita said with a preening laugh. "I'm not living at home now. I haven't been for the last week. You know those McDonnells—the ones I help when they entertain? They've gone to Hawaii, and they wanted me to stay and look after the house and their Siamese cat and the old uncle."

"What's the matter with the uncle?"

"Nothing. If you ask me, he's a grumpy, old hypochondriac. But it's better being there than at home. And don't think I've told my family the address. I don't want the old lady showing up when she's half-crocked and trying to pry the price of a bottle out of me. I phone Lennie every day or two to see how he's getting along. Lennie's a good kid." She always tacked that on defensively, as though daring her listener to say differently. "So you tell him that I'll be phoning him at six this evening, and I want him to be in the house where he'll hear the phone."

Katie Rose fitted her books into the familiar niche between left elbow and hip bone. "I'll tell him if I see him," she said, and walked swiftly toward the wide glass front door of Adams High.

"You can send one of your littles to tell him, if you don't see him," Rita called after her.

There seemed to be neither a please nor a thank you in Rita's vocabulary. "Somebody ought to tell her she hasn't got the manners of a kangaroo," Katie Rose muttered to herself. She even wished she could get up the courage to tell her herself. But she was what the O'Byrnes called mealy-mouthed,

24

meaning that she would never stand up to anyone and speak her mind.

She stepped into a late afternoon as bright and warm as July. These changeable days! She took off her sweater and started on, feeling a little lonely without either Miguel or Jeanie.

Now what was the nebulous tag-end of an idea that had just begun to sizzle when Rita shouted at her. She couldn't remember. She couldn't recapture the same mood that had come over her when she stood by her locker and turned the pages of her scrapbook.

❊ 3 ❊

Wetzel's neighborhood grocery was on the corner.
The store could easily be taken for a house for the
simple reason that it had been a one-story frame
bungalow, complete with porch, until Mr. and Mrs.
Wetzel made the front of it into a store, with their
living quarters behind it.

On the lot next to the store, flush with the street,
was a low frame building with a weathered sign, AL
FLOOD. BODY AND FENDER WORK. The Flood family
lived in an unkempt and unkept house on the back
of the lot which was cluttered with rusty, misshapen
car parts.

Katie Rose saw no sign of Lennie Flood. There
was no sign of any life on the Flood premises. The

same washing which had been hanging on the line when Katie Rose passed by on Monday morning was still there, bleaching in the bright sun. She saw no sign of Al Flood, that wiry, unsmiling man with the lines in his face etched in black grease. Nor was there any sound of pounding or the hiss of an acetylene torch from his shop.

Yes, when Katie Rose wasn't with Rita Flood she could be objective and feel sympathy for her. She could almost forgive her for being pushy and ill-mannered and, for what was even worse, being sticky and buddy-buddy. Poor Rita. Poor anybody, with a home and family like the Floods.

Rita's two older brothers, Bigsy and Irv, had been in and out of Juvenile Hall and the reform school from the time they were twelve. Bigsy, the older, had gotten too old for the reform school. For his last offense—breaking into a liquor store on the Boulevard—he had been sent to the pen at Buena Vista. And there, had met a violent end last summer. The newspapers had stated briefly that, in trying to escape, he had fallen in the rocky foothills and died of a concussion.

It had seemed all the more tragic to Katie Rose because Rita hadn't thought it so. When Katie Rose said, "I was sorry to hear about Bigsy," Rita had answered with a shrug, "He asked for it."

The other brother Irv was in the reform school.

Rita might be callous, even bitter, about her older brothers, but toward Lennie she was as protective as a mother grizzly.

Katie Rose took one final glance at the desolate Flood premises and walked up the store steps. The opening of the door set a bell tinkling and brought Mrs. Wetzel from the quarters behind. She was a plump, sallow woman with her graying hair pulled back into a tight knot, and with sharp, brown eyes behind her steel-rimmed glasses.

Along with the lunch meat and paper sacks, she gave Katie Rose some startling news. Al Flood, the father of the Floods, had burned his arm so badly with an acetylene torch yesterday that he had been rushed to the hospital.

"I was just talking to Rita," Katie Rose said. "She doesn't know about it. She wanted me to give Lennie a message."

The woman's lips tightened. "Message! Why isn't she home looking after him instead of sending messages? He's getting no looking after from his mother."

Mr. Wetzel had come into the store, and stood leaning on his cane. "Now, Mama, you shouldn't gossip." He was always Now-Mama-ing her and, instead of slowing her up, it had the opposite effect, for she had to prove to *him* that she was stating facts, not gossiping.

"Look at that washing on the line, Papa. She put it out Monday morning, and here it is Wednesday afternoon and she hasn't touched it. Why? Because she isn't able to stand on her feet."

"Now, Mama, she has her troubles. She's a nice little woman."

"I didn't say she wasn't a nice little woman. But she's weak. I know she's got troubles. With sons like Bigsy and Irv—" She checked his next Now-Mama with, "You always said yourself Bigsy was no good."

Papa Wetzel had to concede that. "I know. I always said he was born under a crooked star. And he died under it." He limped over and glanced at the scale on which his wife had stacked the lunch meat. The scale registered a little more than a pound, and pepper loaf was seventy-nine a pound. But he said with a magnanimous shrug, "For the Belfords, seventy-five."

Katie Rose knew she should appreciate it, but she went out the door and down the steps smarting under it.

"You can take the girl out of the little town, but you can't take the little town out of the girl," Mother often said. How true, Katie Rose thought ruefully. Mother had brought her give-a-little, take-a-little friendliness from the small farming town of Bannon to Denver with her. The plumber who put in their new hot-water heater told her of his life on a homestead, including a horse that was a glutton for watermelon. The next day he stopped by with a picture which proved it. A querulous, sick woman once got the Belford phone number by mistake. In the process of Mother explaining it to her, a conversation got under way. The woman still phoned Mother and talked over all her problems with her.

When Mother's relatives in Bannon brought her

cabbages and cucumbers by the bushels, she shared them with the Wetzels. They frugally turned them into sauerkraut and dill pickles for their store trade. And, in gratitude, they knocked off a few cents on lunch meat, and gave the Belfords over-ripe bananas, which Katie Rose loathed with a passion.

She had another stop to make. At Pearl's Bakery on the Boulevard. Oh dear, Pearl too was in Mother's give-a-little, take-a-little circle.

Besides her piano playing, Mother had many talents. She let out seams in Pearl's clothes to give her buxom figure more breathing space; she painted the counter tops in Pearl's bakery with a new plastic paint that Grandda, a builder in Bannon, had told Mother about. In return, a grateful Pearl gave the Belfords her bakery imperfects. Sometimes they were cupcakes with runny frosting; sometimes doughnuts that had cracked open in frying.

None of her family could understand why this graveled Katie Rose's soul. "That's the Belford in you," Stacy would laugh. "Listen to the Duchess of Belford," Ben would say in his veddy-veddy voice. The littles had that constant chant, "Katie-Rose-go-blow-your-nose." Even Mother would look at her in perplexity. "Oh, lovey, you're such a *stewer*. You can't live in a shell. Life is just nicer and easier when everyone does for each other."

"For me, I'd like a shell," she would answer back.

Katie Rose entered the sweet, vanilla-smelling shop, praying that Pearl wouldn't, in plain sight and sound of other customers, bring out an unsalable pie and boom out, "All you have to do is scrape off that burned crust."

Katie Rose picked up two sandwich loaves, put down the right change and said, "I can slide them in the sack I have." Pearl merely nodded, without taking her eyes off a gaggle of young teen-agers who were evidently trying to make off with more goods than they were paying for. Katie Rose was saved.

Now she had seven blocks to walk. Surely in that time, she could reach into her deep freeze and come up with an idea, or a character, or *something* for a play.

But before she had gone three blocks, she was loudly hailed by, "Katie Rose—wait! Just wait till you hear!"

It was the three Belford littles on their bicycles. The passenger on Matt's handlebars was Lennie Flood. Jill, who had the loudest voice, was saying, "The unexpected happened—just like Mom said when you spilled the salt."

"Did the school burn down?" she asked.

"No, but just as good as," she was told.

They dismounted from their bikes and walked with her. The three Belfords were all talking at once while the shy, awkward Lennie nodded in pleased corroboration. Katie Rose, piecing together the choppy, excited bits of information, gathered

31

that some wealthy and charitable alumnus had donated money to St. Jude's grammar school for new blackboards.

"You don't call them blackboards," Brian said. "That's old-fashioned. The new ones are green, and you call them chalkboards."

"Every room will be all tore up, and that's why we get out of school tomorrow and Friday, as well as Saturday and Sunday," she was further told.

She gave Lennie Flood his sister's message, "So you be sure and be in the house around six."

"It's a long time before then," Matt said, "so he's going home with us to get something to eat." And Jill, the blunt-spoken, added, "We divided our lunch with him. He didn't have any because his mother was sleeping off a drunk."

"Jill!"

"That's what Lennie said," she said in self-defense. "She always drinks when things happen. He said when Bigsy got killed last summer she stayed drunk for a week."

"But not very," Brian excused. "Just a little bit so she wouldn't remember so good."

They were nearing the Belford corner and the two-story red-brick house with the picket gate at the side, when an avalanche of dogs bore down on them. Cully made for everyone with excited yelps and leaps that rocked each one. But the small poodle made only for Katie Rose. Books, sack of groceries, or no, he found room in her arms while he gave her chin a swipe with his tongue, and the glad whimper that said, "At last you're here. I thought you'd never come."

Mother was at the ironing board in the kitchen, guiding her iron over a white, ruffled petticoat. It was made of muslin with three wide flounces, each flounce ruffled and tucked and lace-trimmed. She wore those full, rustly petticoats under her equally full, rustly skirts for her piano playing at the Gay Nineties club.

"You're all just in time. I'm on the last ruffle, so make the tea, lovey, for us all. The water's boiling, and I'm dying for a cup."

Mother's late afternoon tea and the family gathering at the dinette table after school was a daily ritual in the Belford home. With her O'Byrne upbringing, Mother wouldn't have a tea bag in the house. Katie Rose was pouring the steaming water over the generous handful of tea in the big earthenware teapot when the telephone rang. She hurried into the hall and answered it.

It was Grandda O'Byrne, calling from Bannon, fifty-seven miles to the north. "Is it you, Katie Rose?" he boomed with a trace of Dublin brogue. "I could recognize that voice with a song in it anywhere."

Katie Rose laughed. "Blarney will get you nowhere, Grandda."

"Don't ever believe it, blackbird."

He was phoning to tell them he was coming in this evening on some builder's business. "And Gran wants to send in some of her fryers if you've room—" He broke off to say, "What, under heaven, is all the hullabaloo going on?"

"It's the littles, Grandda. They're yelling at me to tell you they don't have to go to school until next Monday." And Katie Rose relayed the story of the new "chalkboards" at St. Jude's.

Again he broke in with, "Wurra, wurra. All that time on their hands to be roaming the streets and getting into God knows what devilment. And mayhap more old ladies threatening to sue because of their ruining their calendulas."

"Chrysanthemums," Katie Rose corrected.

Grandda was referring to an episode last week when the littles' football had landed in a bed of prize chrysanthemums two blocks away. That in itself, the irate flower growers had told Mother over the phone, was heinous enough, without the three scrabbling through the flowers in their effort to see who could rescue the ball first. There had been talk of suing for damages.

Grandda said, "There's no reason why I couldn't load up the three of them and bring them back here with me. Ask them if they could get ready in time. And now let me speak to your mother, and she can speak to Mrs. O about it."

Katie Rose laughed again. "You'd better ask Gran yourself before you make plans to bring these scalawags home with you."

"Scalawags, yes," he admitted, "but our dear own."

Of course, of course, the littles could be ready in

34

time. They made noisy plans while Katie Rose poured their tea, and sliced Mother's Irish bread for them and Lennie. He ate hungrily, and listened just as hungrily to all their talk of fishing in the creek that ran close to Grandda's and Gran's home in Bannon. The three had long been convinced that the turtle, which sulked under a rock in its bowl in their room, was pining away for lack of a mate. "We'll find us a turtle for him—or else maybe some crawdaddies—so he won't be lonesome."

They wanted to know if Katie Rose would feed their white mice while they were gone. "They like to be chirped to," Jill said.

"I'll feed them," she promised, "but I won't bill and coo to them."

Lennie slid off the dinette bench in his self-effacing way and said he'd better be going home. He was undersized for his age, and Katie Rose saw the holes in his tennis shoes and that he was wearing one green and one black sock. The warm-hearted O'Byrne side of her went out to him. Not sure how he would fare for supper, she spread more bread with butter and jam and pressed it on him.

She couldn't help but agree with Mama Wetzel that it would be better if Rita were home looking after him, than at a stranger's house, looking after a Siamese cat, and a hypochondriac uncle.

4

On that same warm Wednesday afternoon when Katie Rose left Adams High, Stacy loitered at the foot of the old, worn stone step at St. Jude's.

All of the students gathered there were making plans for the bonfire and football rally on Friday night. This bonfire was an annual event, but wood for it was scarce and hard to find this year. Stacy lifted spirits by saying that she knew of an old doghouse they could add to the conflagration.

The football team was already in their suits and waiting for the coach to arrive for practice. Obie, the wiry little quarterback and the school comedian, said, "Tell you what, Stacy, you go with Sully and me tomorrow and we'll load up the doghouse."

Just as Obie was short for O'Brien, Sully was short for Sullivan.

Someone said derisively, "Can't you two micks move a doghouse without Stacy's help?"

"We need her to soft-soap the old lady who isn't sure she wants to part with it."

With that, Stacy's friend Claire nudged her and said, "There's your lover boy come to fetch you home."

A cream-colored convertible with the top down had stopped in the driveway. Stacy answered the wave of the boy who climbed out of the car, and started across the grassy plot of ground to meet him. The driveway was some fifty feet from the school steps, a fact much lamented by the St. Jude nuns whenever the bishop came to visit the school— especially if it was a rainy or snowy day.

Bruce Seerie came toward Stacy in the bright October sun, his dark mat of curly hair still glistening from the shower he had taken after his last-hour gym. His summer's tan was a rosy bronze.

They came together halfway between the school steps and the car. His dark eyes and her sparkling blue ones met and held, and he said, "We were late getting out of gym. I'm always so afraid I'll miss you." And she answered, her voice throaty with happiness, "I'm always so afraid you won't come."

He took her books, and stood for a moment his eyes resting on her flushed cheeks and her reddish-blond hair glinting in the sun. He didn't touch her; Stacy had once said to Katie Rose, "Bruce is no pawer." Their arms touched lightly as they walked to the car, but Stacy felt as close to him as though he were holding her tight.

"Hungry?" he asked.

"Simply starvelous."

He chuckled. "I'll buy that. You're starving and you're marvelous."

Stacy stood beside him, her eyes luminous. *It's true—the unexpected I wanted to happen has happened. We're back where we were before we started calling each other names. Before we wanted to change each other and hurt each other.*

When, how had the name-calling started? She had called him a drizzlepuss because one snowy February day she asked him to let Obie fasten his bobsled onto his car. "No," said Bruce, "it's against the law." For two weeks no Bruce appeared at St. Jude's to drive her home after school. Not until she had phoned him in contrition, and said, "Bruce, I can't live without you," were they "reconcided," as she had happily shouted through the house.

He called her a Child of Mary, and there were barbs in the way he said it. That was because her practice for the May Day rites of crowning the Virgin had interfered with her meeting him after school.

Their latest and bitterest quarrel was over his wanting her to change from St. Jude's to the newer, bigger, and more modern John Quincy Adams High from which he would graduate this coming

February. Too much time and absorption with athletics had put him a half-term behind his class.

"I know St. Jude's is a tacky old school," she admitted. "But I started there in the first grade, and I just love everybody."

"Sure, sure, and everybody loves you. You have to shake names up in a hat to decide who you'll go to dances with."

Stacy giggled at that. She did have an excess of bids to school affairs, but she always diverted one to her friend Claire. Good old loyal Claire, with her thick glasses, and what she called barbed wire on her teeth, was apt to be overlooked.

Stacy had placated Bruce further, "And you know how crazy I am about basketball, and how they don't have girls' games in the public highs. Besides Adams is such a big school. I wouldn't be *anybody*, but at St. Jude's—"

"Oh sure, sure. At St. Jude's you're the big toad in the little puddle."

"Very original," she mocked.

And they tried to change each other. "Don't be such a cold fish, Bruce." This had happened one summer's day when Stacy urged him to give a lift to an elderly man walking along the highway with a heavy suitcase. Bruce, without slowing, said, "That's one thing Dad always dinged into me. Never stop and pick up anyone."

Another time, "Stacy, do you have to be so chummy with that old Greek that sells tamales?"

"How you talk. Delios has had his tamale wagon close to St. Jude's for gosh knows how long. When any of us forgets our lunch, he hands out tamales on tick."

In short, they quarreled because he was conventional Bruce and she was unconventional Stacy.

But she had spilled salt at the breakfast table and had lost no time in spraying some over her left shoulder. And now she was standing beside Bruce on this sunny afternoon and they were in their old, joyous rapport.

"What'll you have?" he asked. "Hot dog or ice cream?"

"Both."

There weren't many boys she would say that to. Not to Obie or Sully who came from big families and were always short of funds. They'd say, "If we take you in for a coke, will you promise not to ask for a banana split?" But Bruce, the only son of a successful lawyer, was always solvent.

He chuckled again. "Where do you want to go? Ragged Robin, Schmitty's, or that new Purple Cow?"

"Not the Robin. Ben will be working there from three to five or so, and he's been on the sour side lately. I don't care where—Schmitty's or the Purple Cow—just so I'm with you."

He gave her arm a lingering squeeze as he opened the car door for her. They drove past the football squad trotting out to the practice field.

40

Stacy gave a reminiscent giggle. "That Obie is such a spook. He was horsing around in Latin today, and Sister Justine gave him—oh, just a tap on the head with the book in her hand—"

She saw Bruce's face tighten. The giggle died in her throat. How stupid could a girl get? Bruce had never felt kindly toward Obie since the bobsled incident. She didn't finish her story, which was that Obie had crumpled to the floor, his eyes rolled back, with his mouth sagging open. And that Sister Justine hadn't realized for a brief, startled moment that he was putting on an act, but thought she had caused a concussion.

Stacy veered to talking about their bonfire and rally Friday night. "Everybody will go up and down alleys tomorrow after school for all the discarded garage doors and such. We like to have wood piled as high as the school. And then I've been promised an old doghouse that we want to put clear up on top. Mr. K told me we could go and get it."

"Who's Mr. K?"

"That's what we call him. You know Adolph Katson, the tailor on the Boul?"

"That round-shouldered little German? I quit going there. Lord, he's grouchy. He'll never do anything in a hurry."

She almost said, "He'll do anything for us in a hurry." Feminine instinct checked her. She must carry carefully this package of happiness. "Yes, I guess he is grouchy. Mom says he's a disappointed musician turned tailor. He played the violin at Dad's funeral. Did you ever hear of a writer named Schiller?"

"No."

"You would, if you ever talked to Mr. K. Anyway, his sister lives with him and she has this big dog named Max. Mr. K says he was supposed to be a toy shepherd but he just kept on growing. She had a doghouse built for him. Mr. K said that at first his sister said the dog was too young to stay in it by himself, and now she says he's too old."

They laughed together about it. He drove slowly through the streets. They talked and sang in snatches. "By gumbo, I forgot I had a starvelous female with me."

"On the twelfth day of October my true love gave to me," Stacy trilled out, "a hot dog and ice cre-eam." Again that squeeze of the hand that said so much. He held it, a fond smile tugging at his lips, even as he maneuvered the car in the thicker traffic on the Boulevard.

He let go of her hand suddenly. He shoved her farther over on the seat with his elbow. "There's Mom. See, there in front of the garage we just passed. She's motioning to us."

He slowed until he found a place to stop temporarily, and waited until his mother came up to the car. She explained why she was afoot. "I was coming back from a luncheon lecture when the motor started to knock. I stopped at Mack's garage here to see if he could adjust whatever was wrong. But he said it sounded like I'd thrown a rod and I'd have to leave the car. I'll need a ride home, Bruce."

Stacy opened the car door for her, and started to slide over to make room, but Mrs. Seerie said, "It'd be better if I got in the middle, Stacy, and you sat on the outside."

Stacy didn't see why it would be a better seating arrangement but she acceded, saying nothing. Neither did Bruce. Mrs. Seerie was a small, compact, tailored-suited, no-nonsense type of woman. She was also the type who was president of any club or organization she belonged to. Jeanie Kincaid had told Stacy this. "She's a gavel-wielder."

The drop in temperature with Bruce's mother in the middle of the front seat was quite noticeable. Not that she ever had—or would—put it into words that she didn't approve of Bruce's choice of Stacy Belford. She was saying as Bruce swung into traffic again, "First I phoned your father, Bruce, to see if he could pick me up at Mack's, but he was in court. Then I phoned home, thinking surely you'd be there studying."

I get the message, Mrs. Seerie. If it weren't for that Belford girl, Bruce would be home where he belongs. Now I suppose we'll have the countdown on how many years Bruce will be in college, and how many years in law school, and how many more before he'll be self-supporting, which is your sub-til way of telling me not to get ideas.

43

When Bruce had driven another block along the Boulevard, his mother said, "Hadn't you better get over in the right lane for a right turn, Bruce?"

"Right? I don't turn right to take you home."

"I think we'd save time all around if you took Stacy home first. She's closer—and then you won't have the trip out to the Heights and back." Harmony Heights was the new and exclusive addition that lay south and east of the university. Hubbell Street, on which the Belfords lived, was in an older and not at all exclusive district, which some wit had once labeled Hodgepodge Hollow.

Stacy waited for Bruce to say, "But Stacy and I want to stop for a hot dog." He didn't say it. He didn't look at either her or his mother, but at the next corner he took the turn to the right. . . . How indignant Stacy had been during their first wondrous infatuation, when Jeanie Kincaid had told her that Bruce was parent-ridden. "That's the craziest thing I ever heard. He's respectful to them, but he makes his own incisions."

"Maybe," Jeanie had laughed, "but not his *decisions.*" . . .

The cream-colored convertible drew up at the side entrance of the Belfords. Bruce came around and helped Stacy out just as Lennie Flood pushed through the gate, clutching the odd-shaped sandwich Katie Rose had given him. He was leaving on such reluctant feet that Stacy said, "You come back real soon, Lennie." He gave her his warm, squirmy smile.

44

Some imp of perversity prompted Stacy to say, more for Mrs. Seerie's benefit than for Bruce's, "That's Lennie Flood. I guess everyone in South Denver knows who the Floods are. Bigsy Flood all but broke a record. He had four 'breaking and entering' charges before he was thirteen."

She even delighted in the cold, condemning look Mrs. Seerie turned on her. "Bigsy was the one who was killed when he was making a break out of Buena Vista, wasn't he?"

"Yes, that was Bigsy. He might have made it, even though it's rocky country up there, if he hadn't had a bum foot. He got it smashed in a motorcycle accident just before he was sent up."

Bruce broke in with an uneasy laugh, "Come off it, Stacy. You told me once you didn't have any use for the Floods."

She knew he was giving her the clue to say, "We can't help it because they're neighbors, but Mom says they're common as pig tracks and for us to give them a wide berth." That was what her mother *had* said. But the same imp prodded her into saying, "Lennie's a sweetie. Of course, Rita gets too big for her britches every now and then. The last time she did, I gave her a clout that knocked her off Wetzel's porch."

A din of pounding on metal all but drowned out her words. Stacy looked to where Jill was holding a pan across the pickets of the fence, while Matt wielded the hammer to pound nail holes in its bottom. The information was shouted out to her, and the world in general, that they were making a sieve for catching fish in the creek at Bannon.

Bruce took Stacy's arm and walked with her to the picket gate. Under cover of the pounding, he said between set lips, "You don't have to act so smart-alecky in front of Mother." And she hurled back, "And you don't have to act like a whipped pup that heels when she says heel."

After the Seerie car had driven off, she leaned against the gate, feeling ashamed and shaken and sick to the point of nausea. The family always said Stacy grieved with her stomach instead of her heart. She had to keep swallowing the saliva that formed in her mouth. Why, oh why, did she always want to antagonize and shock Bruce's self-contained mother? Why did she and Bruce say and do these hurting things to each other?

❧ 5 ❧

At the same time on that Wednesday afternoon when Katie Rose left Adams High and Stacy hurried from St. Jude's steps to meet Bruce Seerie, Ben Belford went to work behind the sandwich counter at the Ragged Robin drive-in.

He wouldn't let himself look out the glass front to see which carhop in drum majorette boots and short, flared skirt was waiting on the cars parked under the roofed area. He wouldn't let himself ask Bess, the cashier, if Holly was on the afternoon shift. He had to go on pretending that he didn't give a hoot whether the girl with the long, black hair and mocking green eyes was here or in Timbuctu.

Every day since school had started and Ben had come back to the Robin to work part-time, he vowed that he would not let Holly's bragging or deriding get under his skin. Surely today, what with all the salt-spilling at breakfast, the *unexpected* would happen. Surely today when Holly leaned against the counter and bragged about how much she could drink, or showed him the wristwatch or cigarette lighter she had pried out of a date, he could laugh and say, "There's one born every minute."

Surely today, if she greeted him with her insolent smile and her "How's Mama's mainstay today? Has she warned you against girls like me? Is that why you're afraid to ask me for a date?" he would laugh even louder and say, "Haven't you got enough suckers on your list?"

She not only called him Mama's mainstay, but the father of the flock. And the good shepherd.

He had been going on fifteen that snowy night when the road patrol had phoned to say that his father's car had skidded off a mountain road. He had come down the stairs to see his mother still holding the phone, to hear her repeating in a stunned, broken voice, "It's a mistake, Ben—he can't be dead— It's a mistake, he can't be—"

That night Ben changed from a boy to the protector of the family. Somebody had to be the stern no-sayer. Mother, both hot-tempered and softhearted, could be wheedled out of anything by Katie Rose, Stacy, or the littles. With Mother working nights at Guido's, somebody had to check on

48

how late Katie Rose and Stacy were out on dates. Mother had no head for figures. Somebody had to curtail spending and stretch the skimpy Belford finances.

But Holly's mockery did something to the fond and easy relationship he had with his mother. When his mother said, "Here's my pay from Guido's, Ben. And here's the bill for the new water heater—and I had to charge some things at Pearl's Bakery. Dear heaven, the way that phone bill runs up," in spite of himself, he'd hear Holly's contemptuous laugh and her, "Mama's mainstay," and he'd say gruffly, "It's all those calls to Bannon. You don't need to gab-gab on and on when you talk to Gran or Grandda."

Or when Mother appealed to him as she had last week, "Ben, those two prissy old biddies down the street are making a big to-do about the littles ruining their prize chrysanthemums. You're better at handling things like that than I am."

Ben had marshaled the three young Belfords down to apologize and had left the irate flower growers mollified. But he took no satisfaction in it because he could see the mocking primness of Holly's lips. "The father of the flock. Ben, the good shepherd."

Her taunting was like a searing breath. It wilted all that had seemed so right, so even joyful in his life. Until she labeled him, "Our dedicated med student," he had delighted in sitting and cramming for a test. He had found a musical rhythm in the words he learned for anatomy; "Endoskeletal, exo-skeletal, dermoskeletal—"

This afternoon, he carried the ten-gallon coffee urn from the counter to the kitchen to fill it with water. Dorothy, the chef's slow-moving helper, was putting potatoes through the cutter for french fries. She was sitting on a high stool because of her varicose veins, and she said, "If you see him drive up, Ben, give me the high sign." She meant that when the boss of the Ragged Robin came, she would slide off the stool and work standing up, swollen veins or no.

Ben carried in the full coffee urn. His hard-muscled arms swung it easily onto the counter.

And then he felt his arms go slack at his side. Holly was at the sandwich counter. "Our clean-living all-American boy," she said, widening her cat's eyes. He felt the old, churned-up, ambivalent feelings toward her. Why? Why, when he knew her for what she was, did one hand feel a compulsion to push that swatch of black hair back from her cheek, while the other longed to reach out and slap her pale face?

"Um-mmm, how I love a muscle man." She always put on a little girl's lisping voice when she was needling him.

Don't let it get you, he told himself. But he couldn't help saying, "Is that why you love Guy Mowbry?" He meant it to be a jab, because Mowbry was the indolent type and a little on the pudgy side, whose hands did nothing more strenuous than drive the Cad which his father had bought for him. He too went to the university. Ben didn't like him. He told himself it was because Guy called him *chum*.

The past few weeks the Cad was there waiting for Holly when she worked the late shift. Ben would see her dip into the ladies' room in her white boots and flared short skirt. She'd emerge in a scanty sheath that showed perfectly every curve. Her black hair, which she caught back with a rubber band when the boss was on the premises, would be hanging straight and lank, all but obscuring one eye. Her heels would click across the tiled floor as she went out the door with her hippy swing. Bess, the cashier, would look at Ben and laugh. "The panther woman is on the prowl."

If only Ben could laugh!

Holly said now, "Four hamburgers de luxe, buster. I don't love Guy for his muscles, but for the way he blows his dough. He knows his way around."

With her lidded eyes upon him, he slid the raw hamburgers onto the hot plate. Part of him was glad that this was the quiet in-between time at the drive-in so Holly could linger at his counter; part of him wished more cars under the canopy were demanding service. Part of him wished the boss were around so Holly's dark mane of hair would be caught back; part of him noted the electricity in it and the way it clung to her hand when she gave it a casual swipe off her shoulder.

She leaned over the counter so that her low voice

would carry over the sizzling of the hamburgers and still not be heard by the cashier. "I have to work till seven tonight. Ben, are you as sick of this dump as I am? Didn't you ever hear that all work and no play made Jack a dull boy?"

"All work and no play *made* Jack," he countered.

"You're getting off at five."

"Provided Les is here at five."

"Let's go some place and have some drinks and dance and dance and dance. I just feel like to heck with work and the whole world."

"Why don't you go out with Guy, the big spender?"

"He's no whirlwind of a dancer. Everybody tells me you are. But then I knew that the first time I laid eyes on you. I've been living for the day to go dancing with you."

He slid the hamburgers onto the sliced buns and said around the pulsing in his throat, "I can't, Holly. I have to take Mom to work. She has to be at Guido's Gay Nineties at eight, and it's clear out on the Henderson Road."

"Do you have to take her every night?"

"Every night she works, yes."

"Now I've heard everything. You're so tied to Mama's apron strings, you can't go out and live it up. Ask her to untie them for one night so we—"

"Let up on that apron strings stuff. I have to put in about three hours tonight to get my biochem notebook up."

"Why?"

"Why? Because I have to turn it in tomorrow."

"Would the sky fall if you didn't?"

He put a slice of tomato, dill pickle, and a sprinkle of potato chips on each of the four plates. "Would it? The sky fall, I mean?" she persisted.

He said, with the thin patience of one goaded almost beyond endurance, "I worked all summer, mucking cement to pay for my tuition. I'm working now to pay for lab fees and books. I don't happen to have a father in the brokerage business like your big man-about-town, Guy. If I fail in biochem, I'd be wasting time and money."

"Oh deary me. Some people slave and slave for a future." She gave her low, insolent laugh. "Not Holly. I'm getting all I can right now. And I manage just fine without beating my brains out. I always come out on top. It's a gift I have."

"Use your gift and take these hamburgers out."

She always came out on top with him because he was the one who was shaken with anger. And she was the one who laughed.

She swung out the door with her laden tray. He poured himself a half-cup of coffee and took a scalding sip of it. So she'd like to go out drinking and dancing with him! *I'm not going to be on her sucker list. I'm not going to let her snide cracks about apron strings get under my skin.*

But they did. They went so deep under his skin that it was like a virus in his bloodstream. The virus of doubt.

❧ 6 ❧

The littles, surrounded by all their fishing paraphernalia, waited at the curb for Grandda to come
for them. He still hadn't arrived when it was time
for Mother to leave for Guido's with Ben. She was
wearing her billowing periwinkle blue satin, and
she turned back to enjoin Katie Rose, "Tell Da I'm
sorry to miss him. Tell him to tell Gran to give the
littles a good clout if they don't behave."

Stacy too had to leave for her baby-sitting at the
Novaks across the street. "But when I see Grandda's
pick-up, I'll run over for a minute," she called over
her shoulder as she hurried across to the brick bungalow where the small children were calling to her.

Miguel came in his Triumph. He walked

through the scene of noisy confusion and said with his owlish grin, "Maybe I'd better not ask you, Petunia, how many plays you've thought up."

"A playwright should be an only child or an orphan," she said grimly.

The pick-up with the Bannon license stopped at the curb, and Grandda got out. He was a tall man, straight as one of his two-by-fours, with a weathered, ruddy face under thick O'Byrne red hair, scarcely touched by gray.

He stood, surveying the assortment of fishing poles, old wading boots, the pan made into a sieve, —even a snorkle. "God's garters!" he muttered.

He filled Katie Rose's and Miguel's arms with the provender he had brought in from Bannon. Eggs, paper-wrapped and packed in a shoe box; thick cream in Mason jars; and the fryers to go in their freezer compartment.

Stacy, holding a baby who, in turn, held a bottle, joined the scene with four small Novaks streaming after her. "I'll just have time to kiss you, Grandda, because we're making fudge."

He folded his arms around both her and the baby (and bottle). He found dimes in his pocket for the small Novaks. "Now home with the whole caboodle of you before the fudge burns."

He wouldn't take time to come in for a cup of coffee. Gran would be waiting up to bed down the visitors, he said. "Let's go, Grandda!" yelled the littles.

If only, Katie Rose was to lament afterward, she

hadn't detained him by saying, "You'd never guess who's coming to Adams High tomorrow. Harriet Cass."

"She is now! I'm after envying you, blackbird. There's a woman with a fey touch of genius. Her *Grab Bag* is a joy to produce—no dead spots to be gotten over as in some I've put on."

As a young man, Grandda had been with the Abbey Theatre in Dublin. Theater was still his great love. He acted in and directed plays in Bannon, and in all the surrounding towns.

"She's to tell us about a one-act play contest."

"Everyone's betting on Petunia to win it," Miguel said.

"And why wouldn't they?" Grandda bragged. "Didn't she write one last year that her class put on?"

Ah yes, if only Grandda had gone driving off when the littles yelled, "Let's go!" For who should come running down Hubbell Street and toward the house on the corner but Rita Flood! She was pulling Lennie along with her, yelling loudly, "Wait! Wait for me!"

She panted out the news the Belfords already knew; that her father had burned his arm the day before and been rushed to the hospital. She added more; because of it, her brother Irv was being paroled from the reform school to help in the Flood repair shop.

"So I got to get Lennie out of there before Irv comes home. He's crooked as a dog's hind leg—and no telling what trouble he'd get Lennie into. It'd be different if I was there to look after him—yeh, and it'd be different if Lennie hadn't already got in trouble, even if it wasn't his fault. It wasn't his fault at all," she said fiercely. "When I phoned Lennie this evening, he told me the littles were going to Bannon. So why can't he go out there with them?"

Grandda looked at the hard-breathing, distraught girl. Though he had left Ireland forty years ago, in times of stress the Dublin brogue was thicker in his voice. "Now what kind of blather is that, girl? Sure, your mother's home to be looking after the boy-een."

"*Her* look after him! I guess she went all to pieces when she saw the old man's burned arm and—"

"Are you talking about your father?" Grandda interrupted. "If you are, then call him your father."

Rita took the reprimand meekly. "Since my father got hurt, Mom's been tippling. She can't even look after herself."

"Then why don't you take Lennie with you where you're staying, Rita?" Katie Rose asked.

Rita snapped out at her, "Why don't I? I told you what a crab the old uncle is, didn't I? He's always taking naps. He hates noise and kids."

"Then why don't you go home and look after him yourself?" Grandda asked.

Rita wasn't so ready with an answer to that. She muttered that she had told the McDonnells she'd stay. She thought they'd be home in a few days.

57

Grandda's deep blue eyes turned to Lennie, who stood clutching a shapeless canvas bag, wriggling his feet. "Wurra, wurra, girleen, I don't think Lennie's older brother would do the boy harm by getting him mixed up in any shady deals."

"Look, Grandda, you don't know how it is." (Leave it to Rita, Katie Rose thought, to call him Grandda instead of Mr. O'Byrne. Old one-of-the-family Rita!) "My oldest brother Bigsy—he's the one that got himself killed breaking out of the pen —anyway, I saw him work on Irv. Sometimes I think Irv might have gone straight if Bigsy hadn't talked him into stealing bikes and cars and breaking into Downey's Drug, and all that. Irv just can't stay out of trouble. And Lennie's such a trusting little dope. That's what got him into trouble with the juvenile court—"

She turned accusing eyes on Katie Rose. "You know that, Katie Rose. You remember how that older fellow—that Gil Ames—talked him into helping him."

Katie Rose nodded, but said nothing. She remembered all right—that rainy day last spring when she had found some dogs locked up in a barn. Her only panicky thought was to get help for them, and in doing so she had brought the police into it. They brought about the exposing of Gil Ames and poor young Lennie. It was not a happy memory. For Katie Rose too had been a *trusting little dope* where Gil Ames was concerned. She, even as Lennie, had been taken in by him.

58

Rita added, "Lennie got six-months' probation because the police knew he wasn't to blame. He's just off it now."

Grandda glanced uneasily at the one under discussion who was still wriggling his feet. "I don't know whether Gran can be finding another cot for Lennie—"

Rita was nothing, if not pushily persistent. "Oh, he can sleep on the floor, can't you, Lennie? And he's real good at helping. You'll help Gran, won't you, Lennie?"

(So now it was Gran!)

It ended with Grandda, who was a pushover for any appeal, loading in Lennie and his lumpy bag along with the littles and their assorted paraphernalia, and turning north toward Bannon with four pairs of hands waving good-by to Miguel, Katie Rose, and Rita.

And with Rita saying, "Now don't you two tell the Wetzels where Lennie is—you know how gabby Mama Wetzel is. And if you should see Irv when he comes home, don't you dare tell him. I've got to get back and make Uncle his mint tea. His nightcap, he calls it—Ha-Ha!"

It ended with Katie Rose feeling as ruffled as a wet hen. "That Rita's got the gall of a government mule. Does she think she has a lien on *all* of us?"

She and Miguel dropped on the back steps for a breath-catching moment. Miguel squinted up at the sky and the long, lingering sunset. "Too warm for October. Feels like a weather breeder."

Ben returned from taking Mother to the supper club. Katie Rose spilled over to him about Rita Flood and her foisting Lennie off on Grandda. Ben only said absently, "Oh well, Gran always says she can't cook for less than six." He stepped around them and went on into the house. Katie Rose heard his labored tread as he went up the stairs.

She and Miguel sat on until the phone rang in the hall. Miguel reached it first. Katie Rose, standing close by, could tell it was Jeanie Kincaid, and even what she was saying from Miguel's answers. She had talked to the printer, and he was giving her an extra half hour to get the dummy to him. It would still crowd them to get Harriet Cass's picture and write-up on the front page, but she was sure they could make it.

"Here, Petunia," he said. "Jeanie wants to talk with you."

Jeanie wanted to tell her that she was having a party Friday night to celebrate getting out the first issue of the *Adams Advocate*. "My cruel parents were the ones who suggested it." Her delighted giggle told Katie Rose that her *cruel parents* were within hearing distance. "To which celebration you and Miguel are cordially invited."

"I'm not staff."

"You're the near steady of the staff photographer, goose girl. And I'm asking Ben to come on over after work. Has he come home yet from driving your mother to Guido's?"

"Yes, I'll call him."

60

And Katie Rose could also catch the gist of that telephone conversation. It gave her an uneasy feeling. Ben's enthusiasm for Jeanie's celebration was certainly lukewarm. He reminded her that Friday night was his night to work late. Sometimes he could get off at eleven, but sometimes the crowd hung on and on.

Definitely, Ben was not his old self.

PART TWO

Thursday

7

Yes, Irv Flood was out on parole.

Katie Rose and Miguel saw him the next morning as they drove past the Flood premises. He was taking something off the clothesline and didn't see them.

"Don't stop at the store, Miguel," Katie Rose said swiftly. He usually stopped at Wetzel's for candy bars to have on hand throughout the day. "I don't want Irv to see us, or to be asking us where Rita and Lennie are."

Miguel went on past the little store and turned the corner. "I feel sorry for the guy," he commented.

Rita Flood was waiting for Katie Rose at her locker. "Did you two drive past our place?" she wanted to know. "Do you know if Irv's home yet?"

"Yes, we drove past your place," Miguel said. "And yes, we know Irv's home. We saw him."

Jeanie's arrival cut short any further discussion of Flood affairs. This morning Jeanie was all ye editor in chief of the school paper, and there was no pixie grin in evidence. She reminded Miguel to arrange for the school dark room so that he could develop the Harriet Cass picture. She turned to study the sketch the staff artist had made of their principal by copying his photograph.

"I did it over again last night," he said, "and if you tell me once more that the ear isn't right, I'm going to put a toboggan cap on him."

Jeanie placated him, "It's really a swell likeness. Only couldn't you shave just a little off the lobe right here?" She planned on to Katie Rose, "In my write-up of Harriet Cass, I'd like to mention you and your Valentine play, and that you're a likely contender in the contest."

Dark, uneasy wings fluttered under Katie Rose's ribs. "Oh no, Jeanie—no. I don't even have an idea. I kept thinking last night about Christopher and Howard saying they'd put their money on me. It's scary," she ended on a sharp intake of breath.

Miguel patted her arm in understanding and concern. "Thumbnail sketch of Petunia: Purple eyes, a questing soul, and a hard wanter. Take off your sweater and then I'll give you your books."

He put the books in her arms, and went off with his disjointed lope. She stood there in all the early morning din of voices and banging lockers. *I was standing right here yesterday when I felt the first small stirring of an idea. I was turning the pages of my scrapbook—*

The bell rang. Jeanie and she automatically fell into step and started toward the stairs which would take them to their homeroom on the second floor. They were almost there when Jeanie stopped and asked, "Katie Rose, do you know what's got into Ben?"

There was no use hedging with the forthright Jeanie, or pretending she didn't know what she was talking about. "No, doggone it, I don't. I can't figure it. He doesn't sing when he's getting breakfast. He doesn't chew me out for taking so long to dress in the morning. I never thought I'd worry about Ben not being bossy."

"He acted so eely last night about coming to my party tomorrow night. For the first time I felt as though *I* were pursuing *him.*"

"That'll be the day!" Katie Rose grunted just as they reached the door of room 215. But she remembered Ben's evasiveness over the phone. It worried her.

The school day was over when the forty or so members of both the Scribblers' and the Drama clubs awaited the arrival of Harriet Cass. Mrs. Dujardin had gone downstairs to welcome her and conduct her to her audience.

The guest speaker was a little late, and the drama

room was hot, but Katie Rose felt an inner tremor like a shivering. Jeanie Kincaid, notebook open and ball-point poised, sat in the seat ahead of her. Miguel, his precious Leica unsheathed, lounged by one of the windows.

Mrs. Dujardin ushered in the awaited speaker. Every student rose in deference, and Katie Rose murmured to Jeanie, "She doesn't look like a celebrity."

Beside Mrs. Dujardin, who had heightened her black costume with a heavy jade necklace and earrings, Harriet Cass appeared a little everydayish. Her gray print dress was mussed, her medium brown hair was sprinkled with gray. She was of medium height. But her eyes, the same dark gray as the background of her dress, had an all-seeing depth and humor and wisdom.

She apologized briefly for keeping them waiting; Adams High was the third school she had visited that afternoon. The one-act play contest for high-school seniors was to encourage interest in theater, she told them, and to discover talent in young writers. "Our Civic Theater will produce the winning five."

Katie Rose's dream clamored hurtingly in her breast. She had already had a taste of the heady triumph of seeing the characters she had created in her Valentine play come to life on the stage. Of hearing the dialogue she had written come from their lips and stir the audience to sympathy or laughter . . . And besides—besides— "There's

68

Katie Rose Belford. She wrote a prize play, and everybody says it's a knockout."

"Your play must not exceed fifty minutes playing time," Harriet Cass was saying. "That means that your manuscript mustn't be over fifty pages, for a page of dialogue runs to approximately one minute of play." Pencils and pens were busy in notebooks. "As for the number of characters—"

Katie Rose was tapped on the shoulder by the boy behind her. He jerked his thumb toward the door, and whispered, "Someone wants you."

She glanced toward the door, the top half of which was glass. A girl was gesturing imperatively for her to come out. Again it took a second or two for Katie Rose's absorbed mind to focus on the interrupter's sharp, insistent face under the puffball of hair. Good heavens, Rita Flood! And motioning her to come out in the hall while Harriet Cass was speaking!

Katie Rose shook her head, and nodded toward the front of the room, trying to convey that she was listening to an important speaker.

She turned her attention back to the playwright in time to hear her say, "Strindberg has only two main characters with a waitress in the background." In the seat ahead of her, Jeanie was filling pages of her notebook with shorthand squiggles. Miguel was not taking notes, but listening intently. Maybe he could fill her in on any points Rita had made her miss.

She tried not to look at the door again. But she

couldn't help it. Rita was gesturing even more urgently. Her words even reached through the door, "Irv's outside. Come on out!" Katie Rose ground her teeth. Come on out, my eye!

Harriet Cass was now answering a question from Christopher. He must have asked where she got ideas for her plays, for she was saying, "The mind, of course, is a storehouse." Miguel flashed Katie Rose a smile that said, "Only Pop calls it a deep freeze." The speaker added thoughtfully, "Every experience, every emotion adds to it. Strangely enough, I find that, with me, an emotional upheaval seems to sharpen and stir the creative instinct."

She paused thoughtfully again. "I can tell you how *not* to write a play. Don't say, 'Now I'm going to write about this or that.'" She shook her head with emphasis. "No, I don't believe that ever works. Wait until a character, or an idea, possibly a scene, clutches at you and begs, 'write about me, write about this.' It will leave you no peace until you do. It's in your fingertips and your heartbeat—you can't help yourself. Don't force it. If you let your mind lie fallow and receptive, an idea will—"

Heaven help us, Rita again! This time it was the girl across the aisle from Katie Rose who nudged her and nodded toward the door. Rita was holding up to the glass door a page on which she had written in large letters, HURRY UP. COME OUT.

Katie Rose yanked a page from her notebook, wrote on it, I CAN'T. THIS IS ABOUT THE PLAY CONTEST. She left her seat, opened the door a crack, and thrust it at Rita, saying through her teeth, "I have to hear what she's saying." She didn't take time to listen to Rita's tumbled rush of words, but went back to her seat after closing the door.

The talk was over. Mrs. Dujardin stood up and took a minute to explain that, because time was short, she would like any contestants to submit a synopsis to her by Monday. "I can advise you whether or not it is worth putting a lot of work into."

The bulk of the students quickly thinned out. Miguel, sidling this way and that, was peering through his camera lens to get a shot of Harriet Cass. Mrs. Dujardin motioned to both Jeanie and Katie Rose. She introduced Jeanie as the editor of the school paper. "And, Harriet, this is Katie Rose Belford. We're all expecting her to come up with something good. You remember I showed you her Valentine play that we put on last year?"

Harriet Cass gave Katie Rose a warm, encouraging smile and handshake. "Yes, I remember the play. Good theater in it. And you have what I call 'seeking eyes.' Remember to use the same stuff life is made of in your play. You have only to read O'Neill, Tennessee Williams—or go back to Strindberg."

Katie Rose asked timidly, "You said that a play would take over your fingertips and heartbeat. Do you know when it does?"

The woman laughed. "Indeed you'll know, my dear. First you feel the yeasting, the sizzling inside

71

of you. Your mind becomes the stage where the characters—happy, bitter, hilarious, driven—take over. You are helpless. You know then that you are only the instrument, that all you can do is hold your material to form. And when that time comes, you know you are a writer, for better or for worse."

With that Katie Rose's arm was clutched by peremptory fingers, and Rita Flood was saying, "I saw everybody else coming out. You don't have to hang around when the talk's over."

Katie Rose longed to hear Jeanie's further questions and Harriet Cass's answers. But there was no shaking off Rita. There was nothing to do but walk out of the room with her.

Miguel came out too with his camera and said in passing, "Sorry, I can't take you home this aft, Petunia. I'm heading for the darkroom. I got one shot of Harriet talking to you."

"Miguel, please don't use it," she called after him.

Jeanie was the next one to slow her hurrying pace as she passed Katie Rose. "Does your watch say four-thirty? Whew, it's a tight squeeze. Wish us luck, Katie Rose."

Rita, who was not at all concerned about the *Adams Advocate* making the printing deadline, said, "Irv will stop you when you go out and ask you if I've already gone. I wish you'd hurry. I don't want him coming inside the school in his reform school clothes."

"Then go on out yourself. Why do I have to do your dirty work? Irv won't eat you."

"Are you crazy? What's to keep him from following me home, and finding out where I'm staying? And that Lennie isn't with me?"

Katie Rose turned toward the stairs to go to her locker on first, and Rita kept step with her. "And don't you even breathe, no matter how Irv pumps you, that Lennie isn't in town. Irv's so foxy, he could put two and two together and figure out he went to Bannon with the littles. He knows they pal around together."

More's the pity. And more's the pity, Grandda hadn't driven off for Bannon just a few minutes sooner. For then I wouldn't have you ordering me what to say and what not to say to Irv. For then I could let my mind lie fallow and receptive for a play idea.

"Hurry up, Katie Rose. The sooner you go out and tell him I'm gone, the sooner he'll leave."

Katie Rose walked reluctantly toward the open glass doors. Maybe Irv had grown tired of waiting and gone on. Maybe if he was there, he might not recognize her. After all, she hadn't seen much of him in the past few years.

Alas for her hopes! Irv Flood was standing on the middle step. He tossed away his cigarette and moved toward her with a smiling and cocky, "Hi there, Katie Rose," as though he were a long-lost friend she would be delighted to see.

73

8

All the Flood children seemed to have come from the same nondescript mold. They all had pale eyes that were neither blue nor gray, and hair that was neither dark nor light, but the color of a worn jute doormat. They were all a little round of shoulder, and they all had uneven teeth. Irv's greeting smile showed two crooked teeth in front, and it flashed through Katie Rose's mind that in any family but the Floods they would have been straightened in childhood.

He and Ben Belford had been in the same grade at St. Jude's before Irv's schooling was interrupted by short stays at Juvenile Hall and longer ones at the reform school.

"How's it going, Katie Rose?" He fell into step beside her, his thick-soled shoes making a clopping sound on the cement.

"Fine," she said briefly. Were those worn Levi's and denim jacket reform school clothes? His hacked-off haircut definitely was. So were those heavy work shoes.

She winced under the curious glances Adams students turned her way. *So I'm snobbish,* she defended herself, *but I don't want everyone thinking I had an after-school date with Irv Flood.*

She walked a little faster past the parking lot, and so did he. He must have left a job at the body shop to come over to school. He smelled of metallic paint. He had washed his face, she saw, but had missed a smudge of grease behind his ear.

"Saw Ben in your old Chevy heading toward the Robin as I was coming over. Guess he's still dishing out sandwiches there. Mama Wetzel tells me he's studying to be a doctor. I always said he had brains. You tell him if he gets the glass for that cracked window in the old jalopy, I'll put it in for him."

Well, he was certainly playing the old-friend-of-the-family to the hilt! He went on, "Got home late last night. Went out to the hospital first thing this morning. The old man's going to have to have skin grafting on his burn."

"That's too bad."

A conversational lapse fell as they walked along. She broke it with, "I have to hurry. I want to look for a book of plays at Downey's Drug." At least, he wouldn't have the nerve to go in the store with her. Not after he and Bigsy robbed it two years ago.

"How come you're so late getting out of school? I saw kids stragglin' out a half-hour ago."

"I stayed for a meeting of the Drama Club."

"Rita stay for it?"

At last he had gotten down to brass tacks! "She doesn't belong to it."

"She still back there in school?"

"I imagine she left long ago."

Well, how did she know but what Rita had gone scuttling through the gym and past the boys' dressing rooms and out the door on the other side of the building, which only Adams athletes were supposed to use?

"Mom tells me she's taking care of some old codger while his folks went to Hawaii. I got to get hold of her and Lennie."

"I don't know how to get hold of her."

He gave her a searching, doubting look. "You'll see her tomorrow at school, won't you? Don't you have classes together?"

"We have the same homeroom."

They had reached the Boulevard now, and Katie Rose halted, waiting for the light to change. Irv reached for the crumpled pack of cigarettes in his pocket and lit a kitchen match on his thumbnail. His hand was shaking so that he had difficulty putting the light to the cigarette.

Then he wasn't as cocky as he pretended to be.

She couldn't help feeling a wave of sympathy for him.

"This is real important, Katie Rose, my getting hold of Lennie." He took a couple of jerky puffs from his cigarette, dropped it, and ground it under a heavy shoe. "I wouldn't be bothering you, but there's no one else I can turn to."

No one to turn to! The words changed Katie Rose. She was no longer a senior at Adams, ashamed of walking beside a scruffy boy just out of the reform school. And Irv was no longer one of the Floods, but someone in distress. "What do you want me to do, Irv?"

He must have felt the change in her voice, for a look of relief replaced the tenseness in his face. "You've got phone booths at school—well, get Rita to phone me. For God's sake, this is no time for her hide-and-seek games." He fished in his pocket and brought out a coin. "Here, give her this dime, in case she don't have one, so she won't have that for an excuse."

He was pressing the dime into her hand and even folding her fingers over it, when a car of Adams students was brought to a stop by the red light. Before the car moved on, Katie Rose saw the curious and staring face of a girl called Walkie-talkie because of her habit of broadcasting everything she saw, heard, or imagined . . . "I saw Katie Rose talking to the rattiest looking character—honestly!"

Irv hadn't noticed the car, or that its passing had

77

transformed a sympathetic and helpful Katie Rose into the one Ben called the Duchess of Belford. For Irv kept on tumbling out words that weren't quite coherent, as though he had much to say and she was his first listener.

"When a guy's just out on parole, Katie Rose, he's on kind of thin ice. Godamighty, one drink, one fight, one telling off a cop, and wham, back he goes to the Rock and Rutabaga Farm—that's the reform school, in case you don't know. Bigsy and I always hated the fuzz, only this parole officer of mine seems like a good joe. He even drove me down from the farm because he said this was an emergency." His lips twisted downward. "A swell welcome I got too. Mom telling me and my parole officer about Rita snatching off Lennie as though I was about to murder him in his sleep. She was always a muttonhead, that Rita, but I got to talk to her. I've got something worked out for Lennie."

She knew he had more, much more, to say but she broke in, "Look Irv, I don't want to be the go-between. I mean, I just don't have time to get mixed up in your affairs."

He stared at her a long moment, as though he could not believe the change in her attitude. Then he laughed, but the laugh was rusty and creaking as though he used muscles stiff from disuse. "No, I guess you don't want to get mixed up with us no-good Floods. None of us are even worth drownin'. The old lady hasn't drawn a sober breath since she hung out the wash Monday. And do you know the first thing I thought of when I saw the old man out there in the hospital with his right arm all bandaged up?" His voice was raw and ugly. "I thought, 'That's the arm that whaled us kids with a rubber hose, so don't expect me to break down and cry.' "

Again he went through the spasmodic motions of lighting a cigarette. "Well, it won't be dirtying your lily white hands too much, will it, to give Rita the dime and tell her to phone me? Tell her she damn well better, or I'll knock her clear into next Christmas."

Besides the fury that darkened his pale eyes, there was something else that Katie Rose couldn't quite name. She was relieved when the light changed again. "Yes, I'll tell her to phone you," she said, and stepped off the curb. She went hurrying across the street and into Downey's Drug without looking back.

Inside the store, she had to ask herself what she had come for. Oh yes, to look for a book of plays. She turned the revolving rack of paperbacks around several times, reading the same titles over and over. There was no book of plays. She bought a notebook to write her play in.

She glanced across the street when she came out. Irv was gone. Rita had said—and she ought to know!—that he was as crooked as a dog's hind leg. He was mean too. Turning sarcastic about her dirtying her lily white hands. It was bad enough for Rita to think she had a lien on her without Irv thinking so too.

79

9

A disheveled Stacy, her cheeks flame red from exertion, stood on the sidewalk with Obie and Sully. They were in front of the house where the tailor, Adolph Katson, and his sister lived.

Mission accomplished. The owner of the doghouse had consented to part with it, and Stacy and the two boys had tugged and pried it out of the earth into which it had sunk. The intended occupant, who had never occupied it and was now lethargic from his pampered life, only wagged his tail with slight interest as he watched. The boys with Stacy's help loaded the doghouse, along with the rusty chain they couldn't detach, onto the flat bottom of the truck Sully had borrowed from his brother-in-law.

The three stood on the sidewalk breathing hard and brushing dirt, grass, and wood particles off their clothes. Stacy kept looking anxiously up and down the street and was finally rewarded by seeing Bruce Seerie's convertible stopping across from where they stood. She said hastily, "I'll leave you fellows to unload the doghouse and I'll go on with Bruce."

Bruce made no move to come across the street, and Obie said, "Your Romeo is shy. But I don't expect him to make a big fuss over me. Shall I tell him, Stacy, to treat me just as he would any other famous person?"

"Don't you dare. Honestly! Your corn is as high as an elephant's eye." But, of course, Obie didn't know that he had ever caused dissension between her and Bruce.

She ran across to him. Neither one greeted the other, but they stood and watched the truck rattle down the street before Stacy said in a tentative, feeling-out voice, "I didn't know whether you'd come to school this afternoon or not. But I told Claire—if you did—to tell you where I'd gone. She said she'd watch out the library window." She added nervously, "She indexes books. She can tell you every single book in the library."

"She told me you'd gone after the doghouse. She said you had to talk to the woman about it."

An awkward silence fell. Stacy filled it, "Bruce, I'm so ashamed. I don't know what got into me yesterday to go sounding off about the Floods to your mother. Except that she doesn't like me."

"She doesn't like any girl I go with. Dad says it's because she worries about my getting hooked before I'm through school. What did you mean about my acting like a whipped pup?"

"Oh that!" she said unhappily. "Put that down to my feeling mean because I was done out of my hot dog. I kept thinking you'd tell her we planned— But that's no excuse— Oh, Bruce, I don't know why I say things like that."

"I wanted to tell Mom that we were on our way to the Purple Cow, but she was in such a dither about her car conking out on her and not being able to reach Dad—or me. I'm sorry about it too, Stacy."

Always partings in anger. Always meetings with apologies.

He said, "Nothing's going to do you out of it today—whatever your little heart desires."

"They were saying at school that the Purple Cow has a special—hot dog and drink for thirty-nine cents."

He laughed. "The Purple Cow it is. If you're real nice, you can have two hot dogs. So stick your shirt-tail in."

She laughed in wondrous relief that the rift between them was healed. "I forgot what a mess I am." The zipper of her pleated skirt was at the side instead of in the back. She righted it and tucked in the ends of blouse. "Yipes, I lost a button off my jacket. Oh no!—not a ripped-out buttonhole too."

"You're about to lose your ribbon."

She put her hands to her head, pulled the dangling green ribbon off all the way, and gave her head and hair a vigorous shake.

He put his hand on her arm and said with surprising tenderness, "I remember the first time I saw you do that. It was that afternoon when I went by where you were baby-sitting, and I stopped to show you how to make free throws—"

"—in a basket fastened onto the garage," she went on. "Remember the little hellions I was taking care of, and how I made four in a row and we all went a—little wild? And you picked me up—clear off the ground?"

He gave a low, exultant laugh, and there on the quiet, tree-shaded street he lifted her high off the ground and up over his head. She doubled over, laughing and choking out, "Bruce, I'll fall—I'll fall—" Her hair tumbled over her flushed face and brushed his.

He let her down again. "That was the first day I knew I—I—" He shied away from the word *love,* as though it weren't in his vocabulary, "—was nuts about you."

"Me too, Bruce."

She held the green ribbon between her teeth and, using her fingers as a comb, swooped the thick, reddish hair back from her face and held it tight. She backed up to him and asked, "Can you tie it—real tight?"

He took the rumpled length of ribbon. "This is like a string. Where do you get ribbons like this?"

"You get them at a very exclusive store on the Boul run by Mr. Woolworth."

Again the magic. This street, with its trees of autumn's copper leaves, its old and tired houses, became aglow. Commonplace words between them had the sound of an endearment; his very helping her into the car was like a caress. Their magic went with them driving down the Boulevard and parking in the crowded lot at the Purple Cow drive-in. Crowds of students from Adams High, as well as from St. Jude's, had evidently been drawn by the special.

In lovely contentment, Stacy and Bruce munched their sandwiches and drank purple punch out of paper cups. Stacy looked up to see the cause of a delighted commotion about her, and to locate the sounds of a dog's barking.

Sully, driving his brother-in-law's truck with the dog-house on its flat bottom, had stopped on the side street that bordered the Purple Cow. He had to wait there for the heavy Boulevard traffic to clear. Stacy nudged Bruce and said through her own laughter, "I'd forgotten about that old rusty dog chain." She slid out of the car, the better to see the truck and its occupants.

With the chain fastened around his neck, Obie was on all fours beside the doghouse in the back of the truck, imitating a barking but friendly dog. In lieu of a tail, he wagged his whole body. And then, as though expressing a desire to be with them all at the Purple Cow, he gave a long and mournful howl, just as Sully saw his chance to cross the Boulevard and went forward with a lurch.

Over the whoops and cheers, the boy in the car next to Bruce's shouted at them, "That guy ought to be on TV. Did you ever hear him imitate Santa Claus in a department store?"

Stacy said between snorts, "No, but I've heard him imitate the bishop."

A girl, passing by, let out a shriek at hearing that, and joined in with, "Obie did that at our house one night, and my dad liked to died." A boy in another car also contributed, "Yeh, that bit about his talking to the confirmation class, and one little kid with the hiccups trying to say indefectability."

Stacy was still laughing when she got back into the car with Bruce. He said, "Are you with me? Or are you the sweetheart of all the Purple Cow customers?"

She had forgotten that he never liked her to talk to everyone around them when they were together. She didn't know what to say. She picked up her paper cup and drained the last drop of the lavenderish, watery liquid.

"Do you want to leave," he asked, "or do you want to hang around in hopes of a second floor show?"

She looked at him, to the count of ten bewildered seconds, before she realized it was Obie's silly stunt he was referring to as the floor show. It slipped out,—"Don't be a drizzlepuss,"—before she remembered she had vowed not to call him that again.

She tried to cover by saying swiftly, "You know, Bruce, Obie's father is out of work a lot—and there's such a huge family, and they're always so hard up. He'd never have any thirty-nine cents for a Purple Cow special. I mean, I think it's wonderful that he can give everybody a laugh."

"So do I. I think it's wonderful for you to have your pals at St. Jude's to provide you with entertainment and me to provide you with food."

Those words slowly sank in. The thump of her heart labored as it pumped through a thick coating of rage. For the first time, she understood how anyone could do physical violence to someone else. Her hands were clenched with a desire to beat at him— yes, to claw his smug face. Her lips drawn thin, she said, *How to be Revolting Without Really Trying. By Bruce Seerie.*

That wasn't enough. She had to hurt him more, and only one way occurred to her.

She took her coin purse out of her blazer pocket and opened it. She counted out dimes and nickels till she had forty cents between her fingers. She put them in a very neat pile on Bruce's paper plate. "There! There's the price of my sandwich and drink. It's the last you'll ever buy for me. I couldn't bear to have you brooding over it."

She caught only a glimpse of the shock and disbelief in his face as she flung herself out of the car, giving the door a vicious bang behind her.

She fled between the parked cars, instinctively taking a direction which would not take her toward the Boulevard but toward a spot where only a pedestrian could leave the parking lot. She made for the alley behind the stores whose fronts faced the Boulevard. This way, no one could follow her in a car—in case someone had an idea of doing it, which she doubted.

She ran, stumbling and blinded by fury, up one narrow, cluttered and smelly alleyway and then another. She had to squeeze her way around a truck that was unloading cartons at the back of a liquor store.

A sharp wind whipped scrap paper around her feet. Her fingers, groping to fasten her jacket, found the torn buttonhole, and part of her mind thought; I won't dare show up in Mother Sebastian's homeroom with a ripped buttonhole. She made for a corner shop on the Boulevard with the sign painted on its front glass window, ADOLPH KATSON. CUSTOM TAILOR.

Inside, the smell of pressing wool and the chemical spotter assailed her nostrils, and she sat down shakily. It was all she could do to answer his "Good day to you, meine Liebchen," with her usual, "Good day to you, Mr. K. How's the battle of the lapels?" Lapels were his particular nightmare, he had once told her.

His eyes squinted at her through his glasses. "And what is this? You lost a button. And ripped out a buttonhole—tch, tch, tch. Take off your jacket."

She forced a smile, "I got all that prying the doghouse out of the ground. Your sister let us take it."

"Why Amelia held on to it so long, I wish I knew. That stupid *Hund* never put his front paw inside it."

He laid aside the man's overcoat he was working on. He opened the shallow drawer he called his St. Jude catch-all with its green thread, buttons, and scraps of the material used for their uniforms. He sewed on the button and mended and pressed the buttonhole. And then he held out the coat for her.

She started to open her coin purse, but he firmly pressed her hand and put it back into the jacket pocket.

"Mr. K, you're always repairing me, and you ought to let me pay you."

"I do. Always the same price. Your smile that warms my cold bones. Today, you don't have it." He asked gently, "Are you in trouble, little one?"

She had an instant's jolting memory of the murderous rage that had slowed her heartbeat, and of Bruce's disbelieving eyes, and the money she had piled before him. Such engulfing nausea swept over her that she clamped both hands to her mouth and started for the back door—

But Mr. K caught her and propelled her a few feet to a small and tidy cubbyhole containing a washbowl and toilet. With the deftness of a nurse and the concern of a mother hen, he ministered to her. "Now it's all up. Now you'll better feel." He wiped her greenish face with a towel wet in cold water.

He guided her back to a chair and opened the door so that the bracing wind could reach her. And he talked; she knew he was doing it to give her topsy-turvy emotions and stomach a chance to calm down. It was something about the Fledermaus over-ture he played, but which needed a piano accompan-iment.

And when she insisted that she was all right and must be getting home, he said, "I will escort you across the Boulevard."

And so he did, a round-shouldered, little German not much taller than she, guiding her through the home-going traffic with a firm hand on her arm. He walked a little further with her toward Hubbell be-fore he said, "Yes, now the color comes a little back. Good day to you, kleine liebchen."

❦ 10 ❦

That Thursday afternoon Ben sliced roast beef at the counter while Holly leaned over and told about the wild and wonderful time she had had the night before. Ben pretended he wasn't interested. He left her in the middle of her narrative and went to the kitchen for mustard. He lingered to talk to Dorothy who, in the boss's absence, worked from her high stool.

Holly talked on when he returned and filled the squat mustard jars from the big gallon one, "The music—mama mia, the music!" His unwilling eye was caught by the swooning look in hers. "You need rhythm in your soul, buster, instead of so much ambition. You'll be getting ulcers like the boss."

Bess, in her cashier's cage, answered that one, "Speak of the angels and you hear the flutter of his Buick."

Holly swooped back her black mane and caught it with the rubber band she kept on her wrist for that very purpose.

Ben was thankful to see the boss, even though it meant that Dorothy must push the stool back and do her work standing. For with him present, Holly would slide the sandwich orders through the small opening in the wall which they called the "Order-in," and Ben would set the filled orders at another opening they called the "Take-out." With the boss at hand, Holly wouldn't be leaning on his counter to twit him about being noble, ambitious, and pure. Or to brag about her hot dates.

It didn't make sense, Ben told himself again. He wasn't blind, he wasn't stupid. Then how could he be both repelled by a girl and attracted to her at the same time?

He was glancing at the clock and wondering how much later Les would be relieving him, when a car with Adams High stickers on its windows swung in. Not Jeanie Kincaid, he prayed involuntarily. She mustn't come here to the Robin when Holly was servicing the cars. So far, he had been able to keep his relationship with Jeanie unblemished by Holly's taunting.

It was a group of the Adams's school paper staff, and Jeanie was not only with them but she came tumbling out of the car and hurried inside.

"Ben, I wasn't sure you'd still be here. I came in to phone the sponsor of our paper and tell him it's really put to bed. He was afraid we wouldn't make

91

it. And so was I." She breathed a heavy sigh of relief.

Holly called through the Order-in window, "Five cokes with lemon. White ticket." White ticket meant soft drinks only, and Holly's tone intimated that this was a no-tip order.

Jeanie turned her crinkly smile on the boss who knew her and her father who was a doctor. "Isn't that awful? We were all so beat after our mad scramble of putting the dummy together and racing through traffic to get to the printer's on time that we craved refreshment. But even pooling our funds, we only had enough for cokes, and this nickel and five pennies for the phone."

"You could order ice water, Jeanie, and still be welcome." The boss always told the staff, "Treat the high school kids right. They spend dimes today, but tomorrow they'll spend dollars."

It was strange, the happy, friendly atmosphere Jeanie Kincaid, with her short, thick hair, her pixie grin, and blouse with ink smudges on the pocket, created in the Ragged Robin. As though all of them rejoiced with her that she, the editor of the *Adams Advocate,* had made the deadline. Bess handed her a dime and took her nickel and five pennies. The inside waitress stopped to tell her that her son was a sophomore reporter on the Jefferson High paper. The chef came to the kitchen doorway to ask, "How'd your dad like that last order of ribs he took out?"

"They were elegant—crunchy and elegant."

All this time Holly was waiting at the Take-out window for the cokes Ben was mixing. "More ice than coke in mine, Ben," Jeanie called to him as she went into the phone booth.

He walked with her out to the car where Holly was endeavoring to clamp on the tray. The window on the driver's side would go only part-way down. "We'll just take the glasses in our hot little hands," one of the boys said.

"I have a horrible feeling I spelled Dostoevski wrong in my write-up," Jeanie worried. "Harriet Cass mentioned him. About his having only one background—the human soul—in everything he wrote."

Holly stood, leaning against one of the supporting beams that held up the wooden canopy over the serving area. Ben greeted the other girl and the three boys in the car. The girl said, "You're coming to the big whingding at Jeanie's tomorrow night, aren't you, Ben?"

You're Jeanie's boy friend, she meant.

"It's all right if you're a little late," Jeanie added. Disdaining the straw in her drink, she took a thirsty gulp from the glass.

"Gosh, Jeanie, it's just that sometimes the crowd hangs on and on."

"I know. But come whenever you can." He saw her turn her bright, cinnamon-brown eyes toward Holly. After a probing look, she lowered them.

The five began collecting nickels and dimes to pay for the order, but he waved them aside. "Forget

93

it. The drinks are on me, by way of celebrating the first edition."

One of the boys groaned, "Had I but known, I'd have ordered a steak sandwich."

"All aboard!" the driver shouted. "I promised Mom to excavate tulip bulbs and her high blood pressure will be a-building."

Ben took the glasses that were drained of liquid. He waved them good-by. He walked over and shook the cracked ice out of the glasses onto the window box of flowers. The boss often said that Ben was the only employee who knew that flowers needed water. He was poking a thumb into the black soil to see if it was damp when Holly sauntered up to him.

"So you're way up there on a rosy cloud because your girl stopped to see you. My, my, my, she's like a ray of sunshine and a breath of spring. Your high-school sweetheart," she lisped. She sang in a piping child's voice, "Dear Old Golden School Days." "I'll bet you have a wonderful time together. I'll bet if you're real nice and chop the nuts for her fudge, she lets you hold her hand."

"Shut up, Holly," he ground out.

Her eyes shone with gleeful malice. "Old rock-bound Ben, he was known as in them days." She was laughing as she left to detach a tray from a car.

He said to himself, "There's something lacking in her." It was the worst opprobrium his O'Byrne kin-folks could say of anyone. So why could she do this to him? Why was her mimicking and mocking like a poison breath corroding everything that made life dear to him?

94

❦ 11 ❦

While Ben and Stacy sat at the supper table, silent and preoccupied, Katie Rose talked. As though her tongue were loose at both ends, she thought. But she had to share her irritation at the Floods— yes, and at all of life and its badgering of her.

"You'll notice our foxy little Rita took herself off where she won't get mixed up with any of her family problems. Then she loaded Lennie on to Gran and Grandda. Then today she interrupts my listening to Harriet Cass's talk. And she shoves me out the door when Irv is waiting, instead of going out herself."

Stacy roused herself to say, "Don't be so mealymouthed. Shove her back."

Ben showed enough interest to ask, "What did Irv say? What did he want?"

"He wants to get hold of Rita. He wants to get hold of Lennie. He wants me to be the go-between, the patsy."

"Help the poor fellow if you can," Mother said.

Katie Rose turned accusing eyes on her. "You always said the Floods were common as pig tracks."

"They are."

"And for us to give them all a wide berth."

"Yes, I know I said that. But now Al Flood's laid up with a burned arm. Poor Mrs. Flood is in sad shape, from what Mama Wetzel says. Imagine poor Irv coming home to that. It isn't right to give a wide berth to anyone in trouble. I keep thinking about the gospel we heard in church Sunday. About the man who fell among thieves—"

" 'Which stripped him of his raiment, and wounded him, and departed, leaving him half dead,' " Katie Rose quoted. She had been impressed by the terse beauty of the words.

"First a priest and then a Levite came along and took a look at him and just couldn't be bothered— so they went jogging along," Mother said. "And then the Samaritan came along and felt sorry for him."

"He had compassion on him," Katie Rose corrected. Compassion too was a beautiful word.

"What I mean," Mother went on, "is that the Good Samaritan didn't know whether or not the fellow had a police record, or if his mother was home smashed—"

"But supposing he did know him and didn't like him or any of his family?" Katie Rose persisted.

"I think he'd have stopped anyway," Mother said slowly. "Because there are two kinds of people. The ones that always pass on the other side of the road and the ones that can't help but stop."

"You mean there's some that can't help but stick their neck out—or is it necks?" Katie Rose challenged.

"And you mean that there's some you could mention who get it in the neck because they—or she— does?" Mother answered, and she laughed sheepishly as though she were remembering some of the times she had. The man who was to refinish Mother's battered old upright piano and who told her such a sad story that she paid him in advance, and who was never seen again. The indigent neighbor to whom Mother had lent the English baby carriage when Stacy had outgrown it—it had been a gift from Aunt Eustace Belford and was roomy, sturdy and handsome. The neighbors, with baby carriage, moved away in the night, so that the twins and Brian had to be wheeled about in a cheap stroller from Sears Roebuck.

"That's all right," Mother defended herself. "I don't want to go through life like a turtle, always pulling into a shell."

"I do," Katie Rose said hotly. "Turtles are better off."

Mother, dressed in her Gay Nineties costume, de-

97

parted with Ben for the five-mile trip to Guido's. Stacy had another evening of baby-sitting.

Katie Rose stopped her in the hall. "If Bruce calls, shall I tell him where you are?"

It was as though a sponge wiped the color off Stacy's face, leaving it gray and pinched. Katie Rose automatically stepped back and opened the door of the small bath under the stairs. Stacy shook her head. "I've already heaved up my supper."

"Aw, honey, you had another fight with Bruce."

She nodded wanly.

"It must have been the fight to end all fights."

Stacy nodded again. And Katie Rose, forgetting completely that Bruce Seerie had once been her Mr. Irresistible, said angrily, "That swell-headed, spoiled, mama's boy!"

Stacy said from the doorway, "He won't call. Not yet, anyway."

At last, Katie Rose had a quiet house for concentrating on a one-act play. She hunted up two ball-points in case one ran dry. She settled herself in the one comfortable chair in the bedroom she and Stacy shared and, with Sidewinder on her lap and Cully beside her, opened her new spiral notebook. She wrote at the top of the first page,

ONE-ACT PLAY
By Katie Rose Belford

and waited for an idea.

None came.

But such a clap of explosive thunder sounded that the poodle burrowed under her arm and Cully scrounged against her knees. The rain came down in a sudden fury. She ran to close any windows that had been left open. But even as she closed the one in the dinette, the downpour stopped as suddenly as it had started.

She opened the door for Ben who had been waiting in the car at the curb and who came sprinting through the wetness. "Craziest rain!" she laughed.

"I know. Like there was some left over from a cloudburst, so it got dumped on us."

Feeling a need to talk to him—to someone—she sought to detain him. "I'm trying to write a play. I shouldn't say *write*. I'm trying to dredge up an idea for one."

"Don't let it worry you, Sis." He said it with the kind but withdrawn air of an adult who has real problems talking to a child who only thinks he has. "You didn't have any trouble doing that one last spring."

"That was for Valentine's day. And I got the wonderful idea of the young men in Rome drawing girls' names on St. Valentine's eve."

Ben said from the second stair, "I've got a lot of studying to do." The preoccupied adult had given enough time to the talkative child.

Again Katie Rose settled herself with notebook, ball-point, and poodle. But why didn't Ben settle down to his chemistry or biology instead of wandering restlessly through the house? Strange, how Ben's bossiness, that had so irritated her, should be the thing she missed. Just as Stacy wasn't Stacy without her bounce. "A star danced, and under it Stacy was born."

She devoted ten minutes to drawing a lovely border of tulips around the page with nothing but her name on it. A sudden and strangled "Oh-h!" slipped from her. Now she could name the look in Irv's eyes that had puzzled her. Betrayal. He had coated it over with anger, but it was there. A look of being slapped by someone he hadn't expected it from. She got to her feet, spilling notebook and poodle. She walked to the window and stared out, not seeing the rivulets of water streaming down it.

So the Good Samaritan stopped and gave aid to the sufferer by the side of the road! Fine and dandy, but he didn't have all his friends, and even a drama teacher saying, "You're our best bet." "We expect you to come up with something good."

Again she felt a compulsion to talk to someone and hear someone say, "I think you did absolutely right to give Irv Flood the brush-off."

She dialed the Kincaids' number. Jeanie answered, and Katie Rose asked if she had made the deadline on the paper. "Yes, we made it." But there was no hooray in her voice.

"I haven't got two thoughts to rub together for a play," Katie Rose lamented. "That Rita, and her having the screaming meemies outside the door all the time Harriet Cass was talking! And then shoving me out the door for Irv to pounce on. I didn't lose him until I went in Downey's Drug for a book of plays they didn't have."

"Mom and I are just sitting here planning what we'll feed the gang tomorrow night." It was Jeanie's way of letting Katie Rose know that their telephone conversation was not private. "I'll hunt up a book of short plays around here and bring it tomorrow." Her voice lifted several notches, "Katie Rose, let's go early."

"Yes, we can meet in the greenroom. We haven't had a chance to talk for so long."

"I know. I've been so tied up on the paper. Let's get there twenty minutes before school."

Katie Rose replaced the receiver. She would have to wait till morning to hear Jeanie's, "I think you did absolutely right."

Katie Rose turned her page with the tulip border to a fresh one. How much had she missed of Harriet Cass's talk? There had been something about writers having more sensitive antennae than others.

Ben was now rattling around in the kitchen below. Katie Rose was suddenly hungry. Maybe poets could starve in a garret, but how could she think deep thoughts when the thought of having a cup of cocoa kept nagging at her?

Downstairs, Ben was walking the floor. He had a handful of stick pretzels and, at intervals, tossed one into his open mouth. She had no way of knowing that he had read his lecture notes:

Endocrine glands.

   1. Thyroid, found in all vertebrates, are paired,
       and on either side of trachea—
without any meaning coming through to him.

"Thought I'd make some cocoa," she said. "Want
a cup?"

His answer was drowned out by Sidewinder's joyous yelp at the word cocoa. "You can have some
too," she assured him. It would be a cambric tea
brand of cocoa with twice as much milk as cocoa for
him.

She was adding milk to the boiling brown syrup,
when Stacy returned and dropped down on a
kitchen chair. "Yes, I'll have some cocoa, as long as
you insist."

Cully ran barking to the door. Ben opened it and
looked out. "Now what do you suppose? That's
Viola bringing Mom home." Viola was the cashier
at the supper club who always brought her home.

All three looked at the kitchen clock which said a
few minutes after ten. Midnight was early for
Mother to return from Guido's Gay Nineties. She
was not only early, but her arms were full. Ben met
her at the foot of the back steps and took a large
rectangular baking pan, covered with aluminum
foil from her.

Viola called to Katie Rose, "Here's something
else." The something else was two long loaves of
wrapped Italian bread and several cartons of
spumone, which Viola handed her from the car.

In the kitchen Mother answered their chorus of,

"What happened?" by telling of the cloudburst that swelled the creek below Guido's night club until it overflowed its banks and flooded Guido's basement. "The last time it happened was in '97. We heard that on Viola's radio coming home. We saw the flood coming, and we all worked like beavers to get the supplies up onto the first floor. The electricity went off, and we had to light candles. And then Guido hurried everyone out while the roads were still passable."

"What did you do—snatch up all the food you could while the lights were out?" Ben asked.

"You should have seen Guido's mother. When he said he'd have to close the place for a few days, here was little Mammina pressing food on all of us— especially on me. You know how she loves to feed people. Guido is always scolding her about giving handouts to her *vagabondas*. She's always saying to me, 'You know, *carézza,* there are many in the world who have empty hearts and souls as well as stomachs.' "

Ben, embarassed by such sentiment, said, "That pan of lasagna would feed fourteen or sixteen."

"I know. And all the way driving home with Viola with the pan on my lap, I was thinking how much fun it would be to have a supper party. Not tomorrow night, but Saturday. You can all ask your best friends—Miguel and Jeanie and Bruce—besides anyone else we can think of who needs nourishment of heart and soul. Seems to me we've all gotten into a grumpy rut lately. Nobody sings

103

around the house any more. It'll be nice to have a lot of people in. You girls can dress up in your party dresses."

"Mother! They don't even call them party dresses any more," Katie Rose said.

"The egg talking to the hen," Mother said.

"These lots of people we're going to invite," Stacy queried. "Do we just walk up to someone and ask him if he's hungry of heart and soul?"

Mother gave her a dark look as she pulled off her heavy earrings.

Ben said uncomfortably, "Sure, Les is supposed to relieve me at six-thirty, Saturday. But he's going to a football game. You know how snarled up traffic gets. I'd hate to bet on just when he'll show up."

Mother looked around at her three children. "Well, well, well! We're just all so blasé. Pardon me for thinking you might enjoy a lasagna supper that people drive miles to Guido's for and pay four ninety-five for into the bargain. I mention a party, and the three of you stand there, looking at me as though I were a mental case."

Stacy patted her hand. "That's all right, Mom. We know you're harmless. We won't put you in an institution."

"That's big of you." Cully, whose ears were sharper than a human's in hearing hurt in a voice, pushed up to Mother with a whimper of sympathy.

Ben and Katie Rose and Stacy exchanged swift looks. Just such a look grown-ups might exchange when a child thrusts an offering of dandelions at them, and the message is flashed, "We must pretend we're delighted."

Katie Rose said, "At first, Mom, all I could think of was how much work a party would be. I told you about Mrs. Du expecting a play synopsis Monday. But with everything ready, it'll be all fun and no work."

"I didn't want you to set it too early Saturday in case Les should hold me up," Ben said. And Stacy, who never did anything by halves, got up and did a minuet dance step, singing out as she did,

> Come and dance at my party,
> I will show you the way.

The difference was that Mother was not deceived. She sat twisting the lumpy earrings in her fingers. "I read that new book you had to read for sociology, Ben. But I don't agree with the writer about urban living meaning anonymity and freedom. He thinks you shouldn't know or be concerned about your neighbors. I wasn't brought up that way. In Bannon, life was hard, but everyone helped each other. And I remember hearing Da say, 'Times are so tough, we'd better get together and sing our lungs out.' A houlie, the Irish called it."

Ben felt a sudden surge of his old teasing, loving protectiveness for her. "We'll have our houlie. I'll move the piano from the hall inside the living room door, and we'll do requests à la Guido's." *Tomorrow—tomorrow, the miracle will surely come about. I'll laugh at that cheap, empty-headed little harpie. I'll laugh and be free—and be me—forever-more.*

Stacy was thinking, *Everyone says I'm like her. I used to be, but I'm not anymore. She would never long to scratch out a boy's eyes.* She said with a shaky smile, "How'd it be if I asked our nice Mr. K and his sister? He's just dying to play some overture on his violin for all of us."

Mother's eyes lighted. "It'll be either *William Tell* or *Fledermaus.*"

Katie Rose poured out four cups of cocoa for the family. She added milk to what was left in the pan and divided it, in relation to size, between the dogs. Sidewinder, whose gratitude was always greater than his greed, leaped up to lick her chin before he gave his attention to the saucer.

I inherited some of Mom's warmheartedness, and some of the Belford aloofness. So what am I, Katie Rose? Good heavens, I'm like a turtle that can only pull its neck in halfway.

PART THREE
Friday

❧ 12 ❧

Ben took Katie Rose early to Adams High the next morning, leaving Stacy to ride to St. Jude's with Miguel in the Triumph.

What a different and unfamiliar personality the school had twenty minutes before the first bell rang. Halls and classrooms were just stirring to wakefulness. The janitor was giving a final polish to the glass trophy case. A teacher was carrying a vase of wilted flowers out of her room. A girl, balancing a hollowed-out pumpkin full of colored gourds on top of her books, explained in a near whisper, "I promised this in art," and Katie Rose answered in like manner, "Pretty." Yet in another fifteen minutes it would take a shout to be heard in the bedlam.

Jeanie was already in the greenroom. She looked up to say, "This book I brought you has a one-act by O'Neill. Katie Rose, last evening on our way home from the printers, we all stopped—"

The door was shoved open by Rita Flood. She came in and, without a word of greeting to either girl, demanded, "Well, Katie Rose, did Irv soft-talk you into telling him everything you knew?"

Katie Rose clenched her teeth. What a gift Rita had for riling her! She said coldy, "Irv wants to get in touch with you. He says it's important. Here's the dime he gave me so you could phone him from school."

Rita took the dime. "Thanks for small favors. But if you think I'm going to, you're crazy."

Jeanie Kincaid spoke up, "I can't see that it'd hurt you to phone him."

"Oh you can't!" Rita flung out. "I suppose you think that just because Irv is my brother, I ought to be all lovey-dovey about him. I suppose you think I ought to be in mourning for Bigsy too. Oh my yes, you two can sit there, all sanctimonious and tell me what I ought to do."

She spat out a one-word obscenity between her teeth, and went on, "A lot you know what I've had to put up with. How would you like to have police thumping on your door all hours of the day and night? I've had it since I was knee-high. Bigsy and Irv. Stealing bicycles, stripping parked cars. Petty larceny, grand larceny, breaking and entering—you name it. Then they robbed Downey's Drug. Bigsy always thought he was hot stuff with the girls, and he wanted perfume to hand out. If you think I shed any tears when they were both sent up for that, you can think again."

"But they got out of the reform school after they'd been there a year for that, didn't they?" Katie Rose asked.

"Oh sure, out-again, in-again. Then it was the liquor store on the Boul."

"But Irv wasn't in on that." Good heavens, why did Katie Rose have to defend Irv to his own sister?

"I didn't say he was."

Jeanie's logical mind was evidently trying to fit in the time chart for the in-again, out-again Flood boys. "Then what was Irv in for if he wasn't in with Bigsy on robbing the liquor store?"

"Oh, that was something else again. You might know Irv couldn't keep out of trouble. Bigsy got sent up last December, and in January Irv took a car to deliver. It was one he and the old man had done some work on. Only he was heading out east of town toward the plains when the cops spotted him. So back to the Rock and Rutabaga Farm."

"Just for driving the car he was to deliver? They couldn't call that stealing," Katie Rose said defensively.

"When he saw the cops, he left the car and made a run for it. He got picked up in Wyoming, after belting one policeman and kicking another one. I wouldn't trust him as far as I could spit. He lies like a horse thief. That's why I'm not taking any chances with him getting Lennie into trouble. It'd be different if Lennie didn't think Irv was so great. He always did. And Irv was good to him—in some ways."

Jeanie, the practical one, asked, "What about when Lennie comes back from Bannon in a day or two?"

"I've been waiting hand and foot on this crabby old uncle to keep him in a good humor so I can take Lennie with me till the folks get back from Hawaii."

Mrs. Dujardin came in then, a sheer, black sweater held over her shoulders by a chain clasp. "It's all right, girls. Don't hurry off. I only have to find some student records for the office."

Rita left without a word. Katie Rose mumbled low, "She hates us."

"Yes, because her life is all thorns," Jeanie mused in a still lower voice, "and she thinks ours is a bed of roses. So she jabs you—or anyone else—with a thorn whenever she gets a chance."

Mrs. Dujardin stood up with a sheaf of cards in her hand. "Have you started your play yet, Katie Rose?"

"Not yet, Mrs. Dujardin." *Please don't say that you're expecting something outstanding from me.*

"Harriet—Mrs. Cass—was quiet impressed by you, Katie Rose. She said she felt a sensitivity in you that many girls your age don't have."

The warning bell rang. Jeanie said as they left

the room, "Katie Rose, do you know that carhop at the Robin—I heard someone call her Holly?"

"I've seen her there."

"Honestly, even allowing for my prejudiced viewpoint, she looks like something out of an Addams cartoon with her lynx eyes and that long mop of hair she has pulled back with a blue rubber band."

"You ought to see it when it's hanging straight."

"And I thought—or had a feeling—there was something between her and Ben."

"Oh for gosh sakes, Jeanie! He's never even mentioned her at home."

"Which could be all the worse," Jeanie said with a bleak smile.

The second bell clanged as they reached the door of their homeroom. "I didn't even get a chance to tell you about Mom's party. I'll tell you and Miguel at lunchtime."

At noon, when Katie Rose, Jeanie, and Miguel took their lunch sacks from their lockers, she told them how the freak cloudburst and flood had closed Guido's supper club for a few days, and of Mammina's pressing onto Mother the makings of a lasagna supper. "To which you are both cordially invited tomorrow night."

"Miguel Parnell accepts with pleasure."

"So does Jeanie Kincaid if Ben asks her."

The three of them ate lunch at a table for eight. While the other five were still in line at the cafeteria counter, Katie Rose went on, "Besides having what you might call the regulars, Mom thinks we should do like Mama Guido does and ask anyone we know who is hungry of heart and soul."

"Aren't we all!" Jeanie said. "I love your mother. I love the loving, trusting, unafraid way she goes at life. I wish I was more like her. I wish more people were."

The rest of their lunch crowd descended on the table with their plate lunches. The conversation turned to the Halloween Hoedown which was the next social event on the school calendar.

The first *Adams Advocate* of the school year was distributed to the students at the close of school. Jeanie's write-up of Harriet Cass was front-paged, as was Miguel's camera shot. Katie Rose's breath turned into a ragged "oh-h-h" when she saw it. *She* was in it. The famed playwright was shaking her hand and smiling at her.

"I thought you were my friend, Miguel," she reproached him. "I begged you not to use the one with me in it."

"Hold your fire," Jeanie interrupted. "We turned in the three pictures Miguel took—the printer wanted us to do that. And he used the one he thought would come through the best."

Miguel was waiting to take Katie Rose home. A member of the paper staff who had long been a devoted follower of Jeanie's was taking her. She called him Robert Burns because she said he had a poetic soul.

Katie Rose said, "Jeanie, you'll understand, won't you, if I don't come to your celebration to-night? I'm not on the staff. And I'd like *one* evening to put my whole mind on a play."

That was the truth, but not the whole truth. She couldn't bear for all the paper staff to ask her if she'd started her play yet, and have to answer, "I haven't an idea yet." Her picture in the *Advocate* with Harriet Cass made her feel more trapped.

Jeanie answered absently, "Sure!—the dedicated writer." Her bleak smile flickered, "It's another member of the Belford family I'd like to show up."

Oh dear, Ben again! And Ben's sister, Jeanie's best friend, caught right in the worrying middle.

Katie Rose and Miguel reached the school's front door as Rita Flood was backing away from it. "Irv's not there. I guess it finally got through his thick head that I wouldn't let him catch me leaving school. If you happen to see him, tell him I used his dime to buy an *Adams Advocate.*"

Katie Rose tugged at Miguel, "Come on—come on!" She had had enough of Rita for one day.

Miguel grumbled as they walked to the parking lot, "She's a skunk not to get in touch with Irv."

"She says she wouldn't trust him as far as she could spit."

"Oh, Rita! She wouldn't trust her own grand-mother."

"If her grandmother is anything like her mother, I wouldn't blame her. You should hear Mama Wetzel moaning about how Mrs. Flood doesn't have money to pay on the grocery bill, but always has it for—well, whatever she drinks."

"Gin," Miguel imparted.

They came to the Triumph which, hidden by larger cars, could never be seen until one was close upon it. With a flourish, Miguel opened the door which for months had refused to open.

"Will wonders never cease!" she said in surprise.

"Irv Flood fixed it last night. I stopped at Wetzel's and I saw him and mentioned about the lock being stuck. He worked on it with a screwdriver and a pair of pliers—and there you are. I went in the house with him when he washed his hands; I wanted to pay him, but he wouldn't let me. And do you know what he'd had for supper?"

"I don't care what he had for supper."

"A can of cold hominy."

"I suppose his mother had passed out."

"Stone cold on the couch."

Miguel wove the small car through the lot and onto the street. This wasn't the way she wanted the conversation to go. If only someone, besides Rita, would say of Irv, "He's crooked as a dog's hind leg," then she could stop remembering his saying, "There's no one else I can turn to."

She asked, partly to change the subject and partly out of curiosity, "Do you know that carhop with the long, black hair at the Robin named Holly?"

Miguel, who seldom spoke ill of anyone, was slow in answering. "As well as I want to. Bigsy Flood used to turn himself inside out to please her before he got sent up and met his untimely end."

He stopped at the Belford corner, helped her out, and walked as far as the picket gate with her. "Thank you, my dear, but I can't come in for tea today," he said with his chipmunk grin. "I have to take Gramps on some errands, and he'll be all ready and grumbling his head off. Nothing pleases him these days. I just don't know what the older generation is coming to."

But he didn't leave right away. He picked up a maple leaf, wine red and perfect, and pressed it on the shoulder of her purple slipover. He said, "Irv was telling me a lot of things last night. I think Bigsy's sudden death was a jolt to him. I'd say Bigsy had done the thinking—such as it was—for both of them. Right now Irv is one mixed-up hombre."

"As Jeanie says, 'Aren't we all?' "

"And Irv was telling me about starting down at Opportunity School last January to learn about transmissions. He said he met a girl down there who came in from a little town out east on the plains. She was taking a business course. She'd never eaten one, and so Irv got a pizza one noontime, and they stood on the lee side of the new telephone building and ate it. He said that Bigsy always went for girls who took him for all the traffic would bear, but this girl worried about how much Irv spent for the pizza. He told me her name was Annabelle and, the way he said it, you'd have thought it was Poe talking about his Annabelle Lee."

She could tell he was leading up to something, and she waited with an uneasy suspicion.

"Tell me again what your mother said about who to ask to your lasagna supper."

"You mean that bit about asking anyone who was hungry of heart and soul?"

His face lit up. "That's what I thought she said."

She knew now what he had in mind, but she pretended she didn't.

"Well then?" he pursued with his impish and appealing grin.

"Well then what?" she bristled. "Mother didn't mean—in case you think she did—that we should ask hoodlums who'd walk off with the silverware. So just get that fool idea out of your head."

"I'll bet your mother—or Mammina—wouldn't think it a fool idea."

"What is this, your day for making life miserable for Katie Rose Belford? You put my picture in the *Advocate* with Harriet Cass. So that in just the five minutes it took me to get my things out of our locker, at least a dozen kids said something about my being in like Flynn. It's bad enough to have everyone at school thinking I'm smarter than I am without your thinking I'm nobler than I am. And so you think I should smooth Irv's pathway! I don't want to 'Be good, sweet maid, and let who can be clever.' I want to be clever."

"Now there's something that's always puzzled

118

me," he said in a conversational voice. "Why Kingsley, who was smart enough to write, 'So fleet the works of men, back to their earth again,' could write a sappy thing like that. As though it was impossible for a sweet maid to be both good and clever. Just look at you!"

It was impossible to fight with Miguel. She laughed ruefully. "Go on with you. I hope Gramps gives you a bad time."

❧ 13 ❧

Stacy Belford always had a finger in every pie at St. Jude's.

This Friday after school, she was in the lunchroom helping Sister Cabrina prepare for the serving of cokes and cookies after the football game tomorrow. The school called this hospitality to the rival team, Cabrina's Brotherly Love program.

They had shoved small tables together to make one long one, covered it with white crepe paper, and then laced streamers of green across it. They both stood back to admire their handiwork.

"Now, how many girls did you line up to bring cookies, Stacy?"

"Ten girls promised, Sister, and I'll bring some."

"Is Claire making brownies?"

"Yes, Sister, she promised. She'll make a few extra for you-know-who." They both laughed at that. Sister Cabrina's sweet tooth was the cause of the extra chin over her wimple, and the extra poundage even her full black habit couldn't conceal.

She said anxiously, "And, Stacy, tomorrow will call for special, loving courtesy." She meant that the team St. Jude's was playing had never played against them before. "And courtesy is—"

"I know." And Stacy chanted out what the nun had drilled into her students through the years, " 'Courtesy is to do and say the kindest thing in the kindest way.' We'll courtesy them, don't worry."

Stacy's friend Claire came to the lunchroom door. She burst out, "My goodness, Stacy, I didn't know you were still here. Your Lochinvar drove up and waited awhile—and then drove off.' "

Stacy only looked at her out of unhappy eyes.

"Why doesn't that young man of yours ever come in, Stacy?" Sister Cabrina said sharply. "I've seen him wait out there in a blizzard before he'd open the front door and step into the hall. What's he afraid of?"

Stacy still didn't answer, but Claire said, "I think he's afraid either you or the Holy Ghost will pounce on him, Sister."

Stacy asked, "Shall we fix the centerpiece on the table now, Sister?"

"Yes, yes, child. You go after St. Jude. while I gather up the flowers."

Stacy knew of course that she didn't mean the life-size statue of the school's patron saint that stood over the front doorway, but the foot-high plaster version. This one occupied a niche in the math room, except for the times it graced the refreshment table when St. Jude's entertained.

Claire walked up the stairs with her and into the first room on the right and she, being the taller, lifted the saint out of its niche. She was plainly troubled about the state of Stacy's and Bruce's romance.

Claire had that rare quality in a plain girl of being utterly devoid of envy for the girls who were more attractive and popular. She accepted her flat chest, her thick glasses, the barbed wire on her teeth with realism and good nature. She accepted Stacy's finagling—so that she was never left out of school affairs—with the same realism, good nature, and gratitude.

"You didn't tell me where you would be, Stacy. You didn't tell me to tell you if lover boy came after you."

"I didn't think he would. We had a fight."

"But he must have wanted to make up if he came over here. Didn't you want to see him?"

"Yes—because I don't want him remembering me the way I was yesterday. Only—I don't know, Claire—I just don't know."

They walked down the stairs and stopped at the

library door, for Claire had more indexing to do. Some of the football players were at the front door, and the captain called out, "Wait'll you see the doghouse, Stacy. Perched right on top of the pile of wood. We'll be after you about seven."

"I'll be over at Claire's," she called back. That was, and both girls knew it, her way of managing that Claire would be included in the car going to the rally.

Stacy hugged the statue carefully to her and went on to the lunchroom. It had evidently been dropped on a previous occasion. One finger of the hand which clasped the staff was missing, and the beard had a small nick in it.

It was always a problem to place the statue in the center of the low vase and still, as Sister Cabrina said, keep his feet from getting wet. "Somebody must have made off with that nice flat rock I had," she grumbled. They found, however, that a squat jelly glass, turned upside down, served nicely.

Stacy picked up her books. She leaned over the centerpiece and adjusted a white flower. She backed up, and rested her eyes on the wise and compassionate face of the saint. Some saints had such a holy, far-up-in-heaven look, but the nicked beard gave St. Jude a slightly raffish and one-with-you closeness. Yes, he was the kind who could understand that, even when a girl knew she should break off with a boy before their bickering turned what was once fondness into hate, it would be hard,—wrenchingly hard—to say the final good-by.

"Sister, you told me once that St. Jude was the saint of the impossible."

"And of the desperate. But that doesn't mean that he's a Santa Claus, handing out red wagons and blue beads."

"I wasn't going to ask him for a red wagon," Stacy said, and went thoughtfully out the door.

She was almost to the front door, when Sister Cabrina called, "Wait, Stacy, wait!" Puffing for breath, the heavy-set nun caught up with her and laid a hand on her arm. "And don't ask for a miracle to drop down from heaven either, child. Miracles, I've decided, are like accidents. They don't happen, they are *caused*. All anyone can pray for—or hope to get—is wisdom to see the right thing and then the guts to do it."

Stacy smiled shakily. "It's the guts part that comes hard, Sister."

" Don't I know it!" The Sister herself opened the door for Stacy, and murmured, "Go with God, dear."

❧ 14 ❧

They were all home for tea, Katie Rose, Ben, and Stacy, much to Mother's satisfaction. Katie Rose had come first with the copy of the *Adams Advocate*. Mother couldn't understand why she wasn't proud and delighted to be pictured with a celebrity on the front page.

"But can't you see? Now it'll be all the more noticeable if I don't turn in a halfway decent play."

"Katie Rose, you're such a *stewer*. You don't have to win a prize. Even in my day, it was dinged into us that doing our best and giving our all was more important than winning."

Life must have been simple in Mother's day, her daughter thought.

Ben and Stacy came and stirred milk and sugar into the strong tea Mother poured them. Mother did most of the talking, but then she had a lot to talk about.

Grandda had phoned from Bannon. "He'll be bringing the visitors in tomorrow evening. He said they're about fished out and ready to come home— all four. I told him about our supper party, but he said he'd be late leaving Bannon and they'll eat before they do."

She added what Katie Rose was thinking, "Which is just as well, because I can imagine the hullabaloo when they come. Da said someone gave them one of those big glass rectangles—you've seen them—so now they're going to have an aquarium."

Three groans went up.

"And I invited two guests to our supper party tomorrow. I asked Mr. K for you, Stacy."

"His sister too? She was nice to give us the dog-house."

"Yes, I asked him to ask her. And he said he would, and that she'd plan what she'd wear, and put her hair up in curlers, and shine up her rings, but that when it came to actually coming she'd back out because the dog, Max, always got upset—"

"Lord sakes," Ben grunted. "That dog's almost as big as a Shetland pony."

"Maybe the fellow who sold it to them said it was

a toy Shetland, instead of toy Shepherd," Stacy hazarded.

"Mr. K will bring his violin," Mother went on, "But, praise be, it's *Fledermaus* instead of *William Tell*. I'll run over it tonight. Strauss has such a lilt —his waltzes all but play themselves." She broke off to sing, keeping three-four time with the sugar spoon.

"Did you ask someone else?" Katie Rose asked.

"Pearl, when I stopped at the bakery. And, Ben, she says she'll come and bring a cake if you'll sing "Danny Boy" for her."

"Why Pearl?" Stacy wanted to know. "Does she need nourishment of soul?"

"Yes, *and* of body. What a time she's having to keep her bills paid since she put in that new glass front, on which she got gypped by a fast, and also a sweet, talker." She laughed softly, as though there were more to it than she could divulge to her children. "That Pearl is such a hopeless romantic."

"Romantic!" Katie Rose belittled, picturing the gusty and well-padded woman behind the bakery counter. "But Pearl is too old."

"She's two years older than I am, you fresh-hatched chick. And that's not actually decrepit."

"But she's already been married a lot of times."

"Twice," Mother corrected. "One husband died, and one walked out on her."

"I should think after that she wouldn't be interested in men."

"Not Pearl. When they're pushing her around in a wheelchair, she'll still be rolling her eyes at the old codger in the next one."

"Maybe she can roll her eyes at Mr. K tomorrow night," Stacy suggested.

This time Mother threw back her head and laughed in hearty O'Byrne fashion. "She's already tried. Sort of off and on, and in between husbands. She's finally decided it's hopeless. She says the same thing about him that he says about Max and the doghouse—at first he was too young and now he's too old."

Katie Rose and Stacy joined in her contagious laughter. Even Ben stopped his fidgety watching of the clock to chuckle and say in his old way, "Women and their nattering!"

Mother said, "Oh yes, and I saw that poor Dorothy that works at the Robin, Ben. So much sickness in her family! You'll be asking Jeanie, of course, but I was thinking it'd be nice if you asked her too."

"I don't even know what shift she's working tomorrow," he said.

Mother poured more tea for Stacy and Katie Rose, and would have filled his cup, but he got up suddenly with the excuse that he had to go to work at the Robin.

He went out the door, still explaining something about Les wanting to be relieved early. Mother stood on, teapot in hand. None of the Belford women spoke of her uneasiness about Ben's erratic behavior.

Mother, still holding the teapot, said, "Stacy, I almost forgot. Your Bruce called not long before you came home. He said he had missed you at St. Jude's. And I told him that was too bad because you wanted to ask him to our supper tomorrow."

"What did he say?" Stacy asked after a pause.

"To tell the truth, he didn't say yea or nay. Something about his mother having the Great Books Club, and maybe some would need transportation."

"He likes to leave himself a loosehole." She said it in such a ragged voice that neither Mother nor Katie Rose corrected her with *"Loop*hole, Stacy."

"I could tell he wanted to know what your schedule was," Mother went on, "so I told him you'd be going to the rally and bonfire tonight—that's right, isn't it? And to St. Jude's game tomorrow."

"And to Cabrina's Brotherly Love party afterwards. I'll make cookies for it in the morning."

On the weeks when Stacy prepared school lunches, Katie Rose washed the supper dishes. But this evening, Mother brushed her aside, "I'll do them. You go on and work on your play."

Katie Rose went to the upstairs bedroom. Usually on Friday evenings, Stacy would be inspecting her cheerleader's white, pleated skirt and sleeveless green jersey for rips or spots. And also grumbling because Sister Cabrina wouldn't let St. Jude's wear as abbreviated skirts as the cheerleaders of other schools.

But Katie Rose found her sitting cross-legged on the floor, with one shoe off and one on. "What are you doing, Stacy?"

"If you must know, I'm talking things over with St. Jude. The catch is, he can't talk back. If he'd only give me a sign."

"You mean like a red or green light? Red, meaning stop, and green, go right along?"

"Something like that. Tell me again, Katie Rose, what Bruce said to you about me. Remember—after that first afternoon when he stopped where I was baby-sitting, and taught me to shoot free throws? Do you remember what he said?"

"I remember. He said he'd never known anyone like you. You were so real. You never tried to impress anybody. You were just yourself. And I said, 'True, my boy,' or words to that effect, 'She hasn't an inhibition in the world.' And then his eyes lighted up like a lamp, and he said, 'I like the way she gets such a kick out of life. You know, when she cries, she cries all over. And when she laughs—' Well, the idea being that when you laughed, he could hear the angels sing."

"Not now, he can't. Now he thinks I laugh too much. His mother thinks so too."

"I also remember," Katie Rose said, "of your telling me that Bruce was more adult than any boy you knew."

"I don't think so now. I think he's stiff-necked." She bent to pull on her pump and unfolded herself from the floor. "I have to go now. I told the fellows to pick me up at Claire's. Come on, Cully, and protect me."

Katie Rose couldn't even settle in the chair with her notebook, ball-points, and little Sidewinder. Stacy seemed to have left some of her heart's questioning in the room. Katie Rose thought aloud to Sidewinder, "I can't bear to see her hurt."

Cully returned from escorting Stacy the five blocks to her destination. Downstairs, Mother was now practicing what Katie Rose thought was the *Fledermaus* overture. And here she was, giving up the staff celebration at Jeanie's in order to work. But how could she think about imaginary characters when real ones kept plucking at her elbow?

She had read once that when Dickens's muse deserted him, he walked among the sand dunes by the sea. And that Holmes, when bereft of inspiration, prowled through the dark street of Boston.

She went down the stairs. "I think I'll take the dogs for a walk."

"Yes, do," Mother said. "You might pick up some coffee at Wetzel's while you're out."

"I'm not going that way." Not when the Al Flood Body Shop was next to the store! Not when she was leaving the house to get away from Belford troubles! She wasn't going to walk herself right into Flood ones.

❧ 15 ❧

Katie Rose started her walk with no destination in mind. But Friday night was the night Papa Wetzel cut up meat for his Saturday's ground beef, and she had often taken the dogs with her for the bones he gave them. It was only natural, therefore, that when she started out, the dogs turned unerringly in the direction of the store.

She didn't call them back. Time enough, when she reached the corner by the Flood premises to stop and reconnoiter.

The night was balmy. Summer was certainly lingering on like a reluctant guest, in spite of the autumn haze of burning leaves, the spicy smell from kitchens of piccalilli, and the pungent odor of tomato vines, pulled up and piled into heaps.

Katie Rose picked up the small poodle when she crossed streets. She was trying to teach him to heel, but it was difficult when Cully ranged widely, chasing any robin, squirrel, or cat he caught sight of.

She came to the corner of decision, and peered cautiously ahead. Oh-oh! There was activity outside the Flood shop. A bright light had been turned on in front of the shop and, in its yellow radiance, Irv was pounding on the bumper of a truck, too wide to be guided through the shop door.

She backed quickly out of sight. But the dogs betrayed her. Too many times had they come this route with her and, in their minds, crunchy bones were the grand finale. They were proceeding ahead to the Wetzel porch. Once there, they would wait, impatient but rooted, until she came.

She went by the truck and the hammerer at a fast walk as though she were too preoccupied with her thoughts to see anyone. The dogs on the porch thumped their tails, very pleased with themselves, as she came up the steps and went through the door.

Mr. Wetzel was keeping the store this evening. He gave her the coffee and, with a pleased smile, wrapped his offerings for the nonpaying customers on the porch.

"Irv's working late, I see," Katie Rose commented.

Her remark would have called forth a voluble paragraph from Mama Wetzel, but her husband said only, "He works hard, Irv."

She couldn't very well ask, "Do you think he was

born under a crooked star along with Bigsy?" She couldn't even linger because his turning off the light over his meat-cutting block meant that he was ready to close the store. And the hammer's ceasing outside must mean that Irv was waiting for her.

Again she felt resentment. Why did she have to get involved with the Floods? Why couldn't she stroll about, awaiting the muse like a Dickens or a Holmes?

Irv was waiting for her at the foot of the steps, flipping the rawhide-covered hammer from one hand to the other. He wasted no time on friendly amenities, but said, "I shouldn't have got all heated up at you yesterday. Did you tell Rita to phone me?"

"Yes, I told her. And I gave her the dime."

Again he fell into step with her. "I stuck around so close all day, I had to let this job wait. I figured she might phone at noon. Or after school. I thought sure you'd talk her into it."

"I couldn't make her phone. I told her you said it was important for you to get a hold of Lennie."

"What'd she say to that?" He stopped by the side of the red truck and, in the bright light over the shop door, his anxious eyes bored into her.

"She said she wouldn't trust you as far as she could spit."

Again his laugh was rusty and mirthless. "That sounds like her. But then everybody thinks the same, including you."

Inside her a voice prodded, You don't have to

listen to his lashing out about your soiling your lily white hands. You told Rita to phone him, so what else can you do? At the same time Sidewinder gave a pitiful whimper and Cully nudged at her legs. She said, "The dogs want me to hurry home because I have bones for them," and walked on.

She slowed her feet at the corner and looked back. She could see him as clearly in the bright overhead light as though it were high noon. He leaned against the dented bumper of the truck, the weight of the hammer sagging his arms and his whole slack frame. He looked bowed down and abandoned and lost. *Stripped of his raiment.* Her stomach was suddenly knotted in pain. Was this what was meant by bowels of compassion?

She ran back, and reached out and tugged at his arm. "Irv, listen, Irv, I'll help you get hold of Lennie. Don't worry about it. As soon as he comes back—" It was all she had breath for, after running back.

She waited for him to answer. She saw then that tears were running down his cheeks and heard the hard indrawn breaths he was drawing to keep back the sobs. . . . Someone, she couldn't remember who, had said to her once, "Yes, strong men cry, Katie Rose." . . .

She couldn't say, "Don't cry, Irv," because he didn't know he was. He made no move to turn his head or wipe away the tears. She said, "Lennie went out to Bannon with our littles. And Grandda is bringing them all back tomorrow night. Rita was afraid you'd get him mixed up in some crooked deal."

"Godamighty, that's the last thing I'd do," he said in a muffled voice. She could see him gather the shreds of his lost raiment—his façade of pride and braggadocio—about him. His sunken chest lifted. Again his words came in an incoherent jumble as though he hadn't been able to straighten out his thoughts.

"I just got to thinking that I didn't want Lennie to be a cop hater like Bigsy and me. You'd never believe it, Katie Rose, the hours we spent thinking up filthy names for them and planning bloody, torturing things for them. But up there at the farm, I didn't have Bigsy to tell me what to think, and I got to thinking— Katie Rose, do you suppose I can stay out this time? They watch you like hawks, and just one false step—"

"Then you watch it. Miguel was bragging about what a good mechanic you are, so why don't you go back to Opportunity?"

"I might. But I'm telling you, that teacher down there don't know as much as I do. All he knows is what he read in a book."

What a mixture he was of know-it-all belligerence, and childlike fumblings and confusions!

"There's something else I been wondering about. Look, Katie Rose, suppose you met a fellow—and like you got along smooth. For two weeks about you eat lunch together and just talk like crazy. And then from January to October you don't see or hear from him. So supposing that fellow showed up, would you give him the cold, glassy eye?"

She carried on with it. "So my name is Annabelle, and I ate lunch with a fellow, and then presto—he's gone. Only maybe I read a little news item about a boy named Irv Flood resisting an officer in Wyoming. I'd say the cold, glassy stare depends on whether he acted smart-alecky about it or not, and—"

"Huh! Annabelle is probably going steady or married by now." His raucous laugh was meant to sound like a-lot-I-care.

"You know where she lives, don't you?"

"Sure. Twenty-eight miles out east in a little town named Plested. She said she lived in the only yellow house in town, catercornered from the only filling station in town. But I never quite got there."

Something clicked in Katie Rose's mind. "Irv, is that where you were heading in the car you were supposed to deliver? Rita said you were going east."

"That's right. Leave it to Irv to land in a mess. See, I'm in this car with a lot of zoom, and I was early in delivering it. But wouldn't you know the bozo that owns it would call up, and my old man would tell him I'd left over an hour ago? So he goes bleating to the cops, and they spot me—"

"Why did you run? Why didn't you tell them the truth?"

"Because when you've been in trouble before,

you lose your head when you see the fuzz coming your way. So I took off like a scared rabbit. And got picked up in Wyoming and—" a shrug of round shoulders, "—the old heave-ho back to the Rock and Rutabaga Farm."

"What did you want to get hold of Lennie for?"

"Like I say, I've been thinking he'd be better off if he didn't turn into a cop hater." He added, with something like pride, "I'll bet anything if Bigsy had lived he'd have drilled a hole through a cop by now. He hated their guts. But this parole officer I got— maybe I told you—Sergeant Henry seemed like a straight joe. He's got something to do with kids' police bands. Did you know about them? They've got a beginning and a junior band, and one, by damn, they call the Inaugural Band. And the kids in it get to go to Washington and march in the parade and play. Maybe you've seen them on TV? And I'll bet Lennie can make it in time."

"Lennie!"

"Didn't I tell you? There's an opening in the beginner's. Yeh, and I told Sergeant Henry about Lennie and how one of the Sisters at St. Jude's is giving him some lessons on the clarinet. You remember that time she whomped up sort of a band? So the sergeant said for me to bring him down to the old police building at ten o'clock Sunday morning."

Katie Rose leaned weakly against the red truck. Of all things! Who would ever think Irv Flood, at bitter odds with the police nearly all his life, would be worrying about getting his young brother into their beginner's band? It was laughable. It was cry-able.

Irv couldn't stop talking. "Me and my big mouth. Here we are, Katie Rose, me and my parole officer riding down from the Country Club—that's an-other name for where they reform us. Time out for a laugh. Anyway, he asks me if I'd like to get Len-nis started on a band career. Sure, sure, says I, I'll be right there on Sunday morning with him. So we get home, and here's the old lady far gone in gin. She tells my parole officer about Rita grabbing Len-nie off so I wouldn't contaminate him. That's a big help to me—me, with my record of cussing out cops, and kicking and slugging them. That kind of talk don't help my staying on parole."

She only half-listened, because she was still turn-ing over many things in her mind. She said, "I can phone Rita. I'll tell her about your plans for Len-nie."

The old belligerence again. "Let her stay and coddle the cat and the broken-down old badger. I can handle things at home without her help. I've got Mother tapering off. You'll notice there's no washing on the line."

Katie Rose remembered the can of hominy which had provided his supper last evening. She said, "Come down for supper tomorrow, Irv. Mother brought home a huge panful of lasagna from Gui-do's. Come about seven, because Stacy will be a little late and so will Ben. Okay?"

He was slow in answering. He bent his head and plucked at a loose edge on the rawhide that wrapped the hammer. "I'll be there. Seven, you say?" His voice was wobbly when he said, "Gee, thanks—thanks a lot, Katie Rose."

To the great delight of the dogs, Katie Rose turned homeward.

❧ 16 ❧

It was the thought of Holly that had drawn Ben like a magnet to the drive-in. She would be coming on about now. She was working the long shift because she, like Ben, had asked for the next night off. She had bragged to him, "Saturday night is Guy's and my night to live it up and love it up."

He stopped at the light on the Boulevard and said, as though he were reciting a litany; "She's a cheap little tramp. She doesn't mean a thing to me." But when the light changed, he sent the car forward with all the speed the tired old Chevy was capable of.

Holly hadn't come on duty yet.

Ben was attaching the filled coffee urn when the

door opened and her man about town, Guy Mowbry, came in, and asked the cashier, "Holly here
yet?"

"Not yet."

"I thought she was working the four-thirty to
eleven."

"That doesn't mean she shows up at four-thirty,"
Bess said.

Guy came over to the sandwich counter and
beat a hurried rat-a-tat on it with pudgy fingers.
"Hi, Ben. Look, chum, will you do me a favor?
When Holly comes on, will you tell her I can't keep
our date tomorrow night?"

"Can't keep your date?"

Guy explained that his father's sister was arriving
that very afternoon from Toronto. His folks hadn't
seen her in five or six years and they would be celebrating with a big get-together tomorrow night.
"Sort of an open house and buffet supper for all the
family and old friends they can round up. And so I
have to be there, natch, as long as—"

Ben interrupted with a nod toward the phone
booth. "Call Holly and tell her yourself." He certainly didn't relish being the one to tell her that the
date she had bragged about was off.

"She doesn't have a phone. Hasn't been in that
apartment very long."

"She ought to be here any minute."

"I can't wait. I've got to hightail it out to the airport and be on hand to greet Auntie. Just tell Holly what came up. Thanks, chum," he said from the doorway. In a brief moment, Ben heard the roar of the Mowbry Cad leaving the driveway.

Holly sauntered in later. She was eighteen minutes late, but she took her own sweet time (as Ben's mother would say) changing into her carhop togs. She paused at his counter to give him her slant-eyed smile. "You are always on time, aren't you, Ben? But then you're dedicated to making a future for yourself. You have someone to inspire you to noble striving—"

Bess broke in from her cashier's cage, "Here's your ten dollars' change, Holly." She glanced meaningfully at the clock. "Lucky for you the boss isn't here."

"The boss doesn't worry me."

Yes, Bess could laugh at her. She did now. "Finding another job might," she said.

Ben could have given her Guy's message then. But some innate decency prevented his telling her in front of Bess, who would exult in Guy's unceremonious breaking of their date.

An hour later, when the sandwich orders slacked off, he went into the kitchen with the full intention of asking Dorothy to the lasagna supper. She was standing over the great cauldron of hot fat, ladling out french fries onto absorbent paper.

The chef asked Ben to taste the barbecue sauce. He did and reported, "I'd say it's perfect. Do you like lasagna, Dorothy?"

Her smile was hot and weary. "After living and breathing french fries and barbecued ribs from here to eternity, I'd like baled hay."

Holly came in the side door of the kitchen and plopped a plate of ribs and fries down on the work table in front of Dorothy. "My customer happens to like fries that are *not* raw on the inside. You might try standing on your feet long enough to cook them, instead of dipping them in the fat and out again."

Dorothy only looked at her in helpless chagrin. She lived in fear of losing her job, Ben knew. The chef turned from the stove, motioned with his long-handled spoon, "Stay out of the kitchen. You step in here again, and I'm calling the Health Department to report that long mop of hair you flip around where there's food. Get, I said."

He laughed with raucous heartiness as Holly stalked out. Ben couldn't laugh. He went soberly back to his counter. This incident gave him more to add to his litany; *She likes to hurt people.*

He waited for the knowledge to set him free. He waited, hope lifting under his lean ribs all the while he filled orders for customers.

And then Holly came to his counter for a cup of coffee before the supper rush started. He looked at her, confident that now he would see her as a flip and insolent carhop—and nothing else. But all the old torment came back. She was still a girl he couldn't take lightly. His hand still had an acute longing to push the hair back off her sallow cheek.

He could even feel his finger tucking it behind her ear.

Holly herself swooped it back and snapped the handy rubber band around it when the boss was heard coming into the kitchen. She scurried out to her own domain.

There was no chance of giving her Guy's message through the supper-hour rush. The lull occurred between then and the after-the-show crowd. During it, the boss went home for what the workers at the Robin called "feeding his ulcer," meaning the milk toast his wife had waiting.

Ben could no longer put off telling her. Instead of sliding an order through the Take-out window, he carried it out to her. He stood where he had a view of his counter through the glass, and motioned her over. She served the order and came back to him grumbling, "I never saw such a tight bunch of tippers. Not even any I could knock down on."

Bess had told him that Holly shortchanged customers whenever she could get away with it. "Any day now the boss will wise up and fire her for it," Bess ended. Ben hadn't wanted to believe it. So now he could add that to his litany; *She knocks down on customers and isn't even ashamed of it.*

She grumbled on, "I've got a pair of sandals on lay away that just match the dress I'm going to wear tomorrow night—"

He interrupted, "Guy Mowbry stopped by before you came on. He wanted to see you—"

"That's just like him. He says his day isn't complete unless he sees me. Here, we've got this super date for dinner at a mountain lodge, and then we'll dance and—who knows? I might elope with him just for the hell of it. I'm not showing my face around here tomorrow at all, *at all*."

"He asked me to tell you he can't keep his date for tomorrow night. His aunt came here from Toronto, and his folks are having a lot of family and friends in for drinks and a buffet, and he has to be there."

Her face had turned blank, and he hurried on, "He couldn't wait to tell you himself because he had to meet the aunt's plane. I wanted him to call you, but he said you didn't have a phone."

She laughed abruptly. "Because I haven't got any twenty-five dollars deposit to pay the phone company."

She left him to unfasten trays from car windows. She wadded up the paper cups and hurled them into the trash can. She came back, holding the trays. She moved close to him, and said in a wheedling voice he had never heard before, "Ben, I'd like to be your girl. Will you take me out tomorrow night? Please, Ben. It's my birthday. I got a new dress specially to wear. Who wants to sit home by herself on her birthday? Please, Ben."

He said around the wild thumping in his chest, "Mom's planned a party. I can't let her down. And one of the guests wants me to sing."

"Maybe you think I'm not good enough for you."

"Oh no, Holly." His words came then, as though they were all stacked up inside him and waiting to be uttered, "I wanted to ask you to this supper party at our house tomorrow night, but I thought you were going out with Guy."

"I'd rather go with you." She laughed in gleeful triumph. "Oh, Ben, you slay me. I wondered how long it would take you to make a date with me. We won't have to stick around with your family all evening, will we? Saturday night everything is wide open and wild. We can go out on the town, Ben."

He heard his own voice say, "Whatever you want, Holly."

"I'll wear my new sheath. It came from Bangkok, and the price old Madame Simone at Simone's up here on the Boul charged for it, you'd think it came over on a private plane. But damn, damn, I did want to have the sandals to go with it. I've been paying on them—they're at Simone's too—and I thought sure I'd have them for my birthday. And I could have, except for all the penny-pinching customers around here."

She paused. He knew what she expected him to say, and he heard himself saying it, "I'll finish paying for them, so you can have them for your birthday."

"Simone is open till nine on Saturday nights," she told him.

He could see through the glass front of the Robin that the inside waitress was at his counter. He had time only to say, "I'm working the midday tomorrow—off at six thirty. I'll be by for you. The supper's around seven."

Back at the counter, he resumed his work with a strange calm. She had undermined all that he had believed in. His power of reasoning, his very integrity had forsaken him. He had lost the *being* of the Ben who felt protective toward the Belfords on Hubbell Street, and who was challenged by the hard grubbing demanded of a med student. He had lost the easy mingling of friendship and courtship between him and Jeanie Kincaid.

He had fought Holly's taunts with anger, and she had always come out laughing. Maybe soldiers, who had fought to exhaustion, felt this same weary relief when the battle finally ended in defeat.

PART FOUR

Saturday

❧ 17 ❧

Katie Rose was up early Saturday morning, which was, of course, the day of Mother's uplift supper party. Mother, herself, was already up and rattling about in the kitchen. Katie Rose fed the white mice so that the onerous chore wouldn't be hanging over her head any longer than possible.

She emerged from the littles' room, holding a dirty saucer between thumb and forefinger, distaste puckering her face. Ben was starting down the stairs, and she called to him, "Did you have a good time at Jeanie's celebration?"

He stopped on the landing and turned a closed-tight face toward her. "I didn't go. It so happens that I'm getting paid at the Robin to wait on customers, not to celebrate the *Adams Advocate*."

Her heart dropped. His prickly, touch-me-not state did more than irritate her. It filled her with apprehension that he had not asked Jeanie to Mother's supper.

Mother took that moment to come into the hall. "Ben, did you invite that poor Dorothy that has such a hard life of it to come to our party?"

"No, I didn't. I asked somebody else that works at the Robin. One of the carhops."

"What's her name?" Katie Rose demanded.

"Holly."

She drew a sharp breath. Then Jeanie was right, and there *was* something—

"Holly? How old is she?" Mother inquired.

"I don't go around asking girls how old they are."

Stacy had emerged from the upstairs bathroom, swishing a sudsy toothbrush over her teeth. "Is she hungry of soul?" she asked.

"I don't go around asking girls that either. Today is her birthday, and she didn't have any place to go, so I invited her to come to the supper."

Stacy, who could neither be subtle—nor pronounce the word any way except sub-til—blurted out, "You mean you didn't ask Jeanie! But she'll be hurt if you leave her out."

A goaded Ben, caught as he was in the cross fire between Mother at the foot of the steps and Stacy and Katie Rose at the head, flung out, "Holy Moses, do I have to have the three of you telling me every move to make?" Which, of course, was the same as his saying, "No, I didn't ask Jeanie."

Mother looked jolted. She would have been more than jolted if she had ever laid eyes on the carhop with the lank hair and the cat's eyes, Katie Rose thought angrily. She couldn't help saying, out of loyalty to Jeanie, "As long as it's her birthday, maybe she'll comb her hair."

"Oh, it's *that* one!" said Stacy.

Ben stalked on down the stairs. And the inauspicious Saturday got under way.

Katie Rose had told Mother last evening about her encounter with Irv, of his confusions, and his plans for Lennie and the police band. "So I invited him to come to the supper party."

"I'm glad you did. He can take Lennie home with him."

This morning, Mother, her first cup of coffee in hand, told Stacy and Ben about Irv's coming. She added, "Katie Rose, I think Irv feels hurt at Rita and her cold-shouldering him. So when you phone her, ask her to the party too."

"Oh no!"

"Maybe she can't leave the old uncle," Stacy said.

"If she comes," Katie Rose predicted, "she'll take one look at Irv, and the fireworks will start."

Mother looked slightly daunted. But she took a long sip of coffee, and said, "That's all right too. I've handled enough fightin' Irish in my time. I can manage the fightin' Floods."

No, nothing could daunt Mother for long. On her second cup of coffee, she said, "Pearl is going to bring a cake—remember, Ben? As long as it's

Holly's birthday, I'll phone Pearl and ask her to put 'Happy Birthday, Holly' on it."

Ben squirmed in discomfort. "No, no, don't bother Pearl. No use making a production out of it."

Stacy was like Mother in that she always wanted every one around her to be happy. "I'll tell you what, Ben. At school, we trim cakes with these little-bitty gumdrops. I'll pick up some at Downey's Drug, and I'll get home in time to spell out 'Happy Birthday, Holly' on Pearl's cake."

"That'll be nice," Mother said.

That'll be just ducky, Katie Rose thought.

Stacy's friend Claire came, loaded with ingredients for the baking of cookies with Stacy. Mother asked Ben to take her shopping. "I want to get a red-checked cloth to spread on the sideboard, and napkins to match. And red candles. Just like downtown!" she said gaily.

It was a Saturday morning ritual for either Jeanie or Katie Rose to phone the other. Several times Katie Rose picked up the phone to dial the Kincaid number, and then put it down. How could she talk to her without giving it away that Ben was bringing Holly to the lasagna supper? Mother, troubled over it too, suggested Katie Rose tell Jeanie that Ben had only asked her because it was her birthday, and he'd felt sorry for any girl who had no place to go. But Katie Rose knew Jeanie enough to know that she wouldn't swallow that.

It was Jeanie who telephoned Katie Rose. And in

her direct way, said, "Ben didn't show up last night. I thought I might as well know the worst. Who did he ask to your doings tonight?"

Katie Rose stammered, "He—well, Mom thought it'd be nice if he asked Dorothy— You know, she works in the kitchen at the Robin, and she has a hard life—and varicose veins—"

"Goose girl, let Dorothy's varicose veins lay. He asked Holly, didn't he? I felt it in my bones."

" He said it was her birthday, and she didn't have any place to go. But I think it's downright, stinkin' mean of him. I don't know whether Bruce will come or not, because things are all wrong with him and Stacy. I wish Mom had never got her grand idea about a supper party—"

"Don't let her down, Katie Rose," Jeanie interrupted. "Her idea of breaking bread, and singing, and fellowship is good. It's wonderful. It's just that human nature is so unpredictable."

Katie Rose was close to tears. "I'm so mad at Ben, Jeanie. I wish you'd chuck him out of your life and never give him a thought. Let him have his Holly." And she voiced the same thought she had about Stacy the evening before, "I can't bear to see you hurt."

Jeanie's voice was gentle, "I know you can't, hon. It always hurts to be jilted. I'll tell you something else. I don't want Ben hurt. You know what Rita said about not trusting Irv as far as she could spit? That's the way I feel about Holly."

"You wouldn't be wrong about her, but Rita was

155

about Irv." And again Katie Rose told of her meeting with him, and of her asking him to the supper. "And now I have to hunt up a telephone number Rita left with me the night she foisted Lennie off on Grandda. Mom thinks we should ask her too—sort of cementing relations between her and Irv. And won't she be a great addition!"

Even Jeanie, the jilted, chuckled at that.

They would have talked on longer, but Stacy and Claire called to Katie Rose for help. The first panful of Stacy's sour cream cookies for the Brotherly Love party had run all over the pan. They usually did, because the cream Grandda brought in from Bannon was thicker and richer than the cream the recipe called for.

Miguel came when Katie Rose was helping the cooks work more flour into the dough. "I'm psychic," he said. "I always know when there are cookies that aren't good enough for the parlor trade."

Katie Rose told him, "I can't find the phone number Rita left last Wednesday night. And I can never find the right McDonnell in the phone book when I don't know the address or initial. So I'm saved from asking our little ray of sunshine."

But Miguel remembered that she had thrust the paper, with the phone number on it, into the pocket of the skirt she had been wearing that night. And that was where she found it.

Miguel's enthusiasm for the evening was equal to Mother's. "I'll have you know the Belford lasagna supper party is the talk of the town. I stop at Pearl's bakery to get bread, and she tells me about it. She asked me to bring the cake down for her. And when I tell Gramps about wanting to wear a plaid shirt and handlebar mustache like the waiters at Guido's, he hunts up a red plaid shirt for me. I'm on my way over here with Pearl's cake, when Irv Flood stops work on a car and hails me. And tells me he's to be one of the guests. Your being good to him, sweet maid, will do more reforming than any of his stays in the reform school."

"The awful part of it is, I'm not good, Miguel. I don't want to do these things. I'd like to pull myself in like a turtle because I'm so afraid of getting it in the neck. Which would be perfect, except for a soft streak that won't let me pull in all the way. Old half-and-half Katie Rose. If I'd been in the Good Samaritan's place, I'd have gone riding by lickety-split—"

"And then you'd have turned and gone back."

"Yes, mumbling under my breath. So don't be thinking of me as good all the way through."

"I always think of you as the first person I met in Denver, when I was hungry and broke. And you fed me—remember? You band-aided my wounds and offered me your baby-sitting money for a haircut? How could I help falling in love with you, Katie Petunia? Besides being psychic about runny cookies and lost phone numbers, I'm psychic about you. You haven't got an idea for a play yet, have you?"

She shook her head. "And that's not all. I'm giving up. I've decided that that Valentine play I wrote was a fluke. And that I'm not the creative type. I wonder now why I ever thought I was in the first place."

"I read this piece about Shakespeare once. How he thought he could never write another play. How one night he rode on horseback through a heavy rainstorm in such despair he was hardly conscious of the thunder and lightning crackling around him. He reached an inn, soaking wet, exhausted, and chilled to the bone. But before he was even dried out in front of the fire, visions took over his mind. He began to see a storm-tossed ship, and an island, and all sorts of people. He reached for paper and, I suppose, a quill pen, and wrote down the title of his next play. It was *The Tempest*."

"That should build up my ego, but I'm no Shakespeare. Speaking of tempests, would you like to call one for me named Rita? I'm just dreading it."

"No, you call her. I'm on my way. Among other things, I have to find or fashion a mustache for the big event tonight."

Katie Rose dialed the number Rita had left. She listened to the buzzing: six-seven-eight—

A man's testy voice said, "Hello. Hello."

"I'd like to speak to Rita Flood, please."

"Rita? Rita? Oh yes, Rita." The receiver was clunked down with a bang on some resting place. Katie Rose heard his outraged calling of, "Rita! Someone wants you on the phone," and then a deep, scolding rumble in the background.

Rita said hello as though she had run some distance.

"It's Katie Rose, Rita, and I just phoned to ask you—"

Rita spoke with low vehemence into the mouthpiece, "Wouldn't you know! I was down in the basement washing, and the old uncle was taking a nap. Here, I've been buttering him up for days just to keep him in a good humor so I could bring Lennie here when he comes back. And then you phone and wake him up, and there's nothing that makes the old fellow so hopping mad. I could wring your neck, Katie Rose."

That did it. Katie Rose had been mealy-mouthed through Rita's interrupting Harriet Cass's talk, and through her riling "Did Irv soft-talk you into telling him everything you knew?" But now Katie Rose drew a long, jagged breath and said in a very distinct voice, "You can stop worrying about buttering up the old uncle. Because Lennie won't be staying there with you."

Rita broke in with an angry stammer, and Katie Rose said, "Just hush. Just listen for a change. Lennie is coming in this evening with Grandda, and then he'll go home with Irv. Because Irv has already made plans for getting him into the police band. He's taking him down at ten in the morning. Irv wanted your help because he wants Lennie to look presentable when he takes him. I asked Irv to come to a supper party this evening, and Mom said for me to ask you too. And so I'm inviting you to come on one condition: that you won't make life miserable for everyone else."

She waited not for an answer so much as for an explosion. Neither came. She finally asked, "Are you still there, Rita?"

The voice that answered was both as awed and as incoherent as her brother Irv's, "The Sister at St. Jude's always said Lennie had an ear for music. I've been planning on getting him some clothes when the folks here come home and pay me. I'd like to come to your supper party. I wish the McDonnells would get back. Didn't I say all the time that Irv would have been all right if it hadn't been for Bigsy?"

Katie Rose stifled a laugh at that last remark. Human beings were certainly unpredictable, as Jeanie said. "The supper's at seven, Rita," she said, and was surprised at how much of her rancor had fled.

The cooky bakers in the kitchen were calling to her again. This time they needed help in finding boxes for packing their cookies.

"I'll be home as early as I can to help with the party," Stacy said.

"There's not much to do. So if Bruce picks you up at St. Jude's—"

"I'm betting he will," Claire asserted. "I'll watch for him."

"You needn't hurry home," Katie Rose said. "Take your time in fighting it out, or making it up. Any sign yet?"

Stacy shook her head. "Nary a one."

It was past noon when the Belford Chevy stopped at the side of the house. Ben had time only to let Mother and her bundles out before driving on to the Robin. She called after him, "Get home in time this evening to help move the piano into the living room."

He had no sooner driven off, than a car, its green and white streamers whipping in the rising wind, stopped for Stacy and Claire. It was already well filled, and Katie Rose and Mother watched the back-seat passengers pile up on each other to make room for Claire and her box of cookies, and for Stacy in her cheerleader green and white, with another box of cookies and her megaphone.

Mother was happily exultant over her purchases. "The thing that took us so long was hunting for a red-checked tablecloth and napkins. I couldn't find any already made up but look, I bought the material."

She unwrapped and shook out the great swath of red-checked material. She nodded toward the portable sewing machine that always sat on one end of the dining table, "Thread it with red, lovey. We won't have any time for fringing or hemming by hand." She reached for the scissors. "I'll cut them out, and you start hemming. It won't take us any time at all."

That remark proved slightly optimistic. It took until four o'clock, what with repeated rethreading of the bobbin, answering the phone and door, mak-

ing tea, and drinking it along with the runny cookies Stacy had left. And with an unexpected guest arriving.

It was Rita Flood. But a Rita who was not her
usual brassy, blatant self. She looked flayed by the
wind, tired and discouraged. She had walked all the
way to the shopping center and bought a blue,
ribbed T shirt for Lennie to wear for his tryout tomorrow.

"I thought I'd have enough to buy him socks too,
but everything's gone up. So you give the T shirt to
him or Irv tonight. I can't come."

"Why can't you?"

"Because the old uncle is just plain, old-fogy
mean." Rita eased her feet out of her run-over
pumps and wriggled her bare toes. "First, he said he
couldn't sleep if he knew I was out. And he goes to
bed about eight. Then he says the Siamese cat yowls
when someone isn't there—besides him—to keep it
company. And the yowling upsets him."

"He's easily upset," Mother put in.

"You're telling me! But, anyway, we heard today
that the folks will be back from Hawaii on Monday,
so then I can go home. You will tell Irv, will you?
And now I have to go back and cook uncle his five
o'clock, three-minute egg."

She turned at the door, and added with the can-
dor and wistfulness that showed only occasionally,
and which kept Katie Rose from hating her en-
tirely, "I was never asked to a supper party before. I
never ate where they had red candles on the table."

Katie Rose's remark about this party being all fun and no work had been slightly optimistic too. The portable machine had to be put away, the table and sideboard cleaned off, the vacuum run, the hemmed squares and the large, red-checked rectangle pressed. And the kitchen! Katie Rose grumbled imprecations against Stacy and Claire all the while she wiped up spilled flour and washed bowls and utensils they had left soaking in the sink.

When the hall clock struck six-thirty, she and Mother looked at each other, aghast. "I'll light the oven for the lasagna before I shower," Katie Rose said.

"Wear your party dress—pardon me, your stardust dress. I don't have anything dressy and festive, except my Gay Nineties ones with leg o' mutton sleeves. Do you suppose I'd look corny?"

"Of course not. Isn't this a Belford night-club party? Wear the periwinkle blue that Miguel likes."

❧ 18 ❧

Sister Cabrina's Brotherly Love party had begun
to thin out. Stacy stood at the long table, dispensing
Cokes, cookies, smiles, and handshakes. But no
more conversation than she could help because she
was hoarse from cheerleading.

Claire came up to her and said in a low voice,
"He's out there." Both girls turned their heads to
locate Sister Cabrina. She was across the room talking to the coach of the visiting team. Claire said,
"I'll take over the bottled goods—you go ahead. Uh-
uh, don't take your megaphone or she'll notice you.
I'll look after it."

Stacy eased herself out the lunchroom door. She
ran down the hall and pushed through the heavy

front door. A strong wind met her and fanned out her white, pleated skirt as she went down the steps.

Bruce was waiting beside his car. He started toward her, looking so wretched and unsure that she broke into a run. They both stopped short a foot or two of each other, each with a dubious and shamed smile. She said with a ragged laugh, "I didn't know whether you were speaking to me or not. Don't mind my croaky voice. Let me apologize first."

"No, let me. I don't know what made me say what I did about buying you something to eat. Good grief, Stacy, you know what a kick I get out of hearing you say you're starvelous. And then for you to bang the money back at me and jump out of the car. I never had anything hurt me so."

"I'm sorry, Bruce. I've been hating myself ever since. I don't know why—it just hit me wrong. I'm sorry."

The times, the times they had said, "I'm sorry" to each other. It had seemed the magic way to sweep out old irritations and resentments. Or was it only sweeping them, like dirt, under the rug?

He helped her into the car and fastened the seat belt around her. He said, "I wonder if they have locks for seat belt." They laughed together, and the laugh eased their tenseness.

"Open the glove compartment," he said. "There's something for you—in the gray store envelope."

In the gray envelope, and further enshrouded in

white tissue paper, were five lengths of green ribbon. "For your hair," he said.

He had gone not to the dime store but to a department store in University Hills. Stacy drew a deep admiring breath and ran her fingers over the satiny finish. "Such loverly, loverly ribbons. Mrs. Woolworth, and none of her children, and none of her grandchildren ever peddled such beautiful ribbons."

He beamed at her pleasure. "I told the clerk I wanted one for every school day. It was the best they had."

"Can I wear one now?"

"Sure. I'll tie it for you."

He did. He adjusted the car mirror so she could admire herself in it. He started the car and looked fondly, happily down at her. "You say where."

"Downey's Drug."

"All we can get there is Coke."

"And cough drops."

"I know just the kind to help your throat. But look, starveling, let me make up for that other afternoon. Let me get you pizza or fried chicken."

"Bruce, you're sweet. But I'm already full of cookies and brotherly love. I'd like to go to Downey's. Remember when we first knew each other, how we'd meet there and sit in the corner booth?" She laughed in low remembrance. "And a lot of times people would tell you or me they saw us there. But we never saw them."

He chuckled too. "We never saw anybody but each other."

The old magic is back, St. Jude. Maybe this time it will last. Maybe I was crazy to think we had to break up. Maybe I don't need to bother you about us any more.

Bruce drove past the drugstore and turned the corner to find a place to park. He came around the car and opened the door for her. He said, "That's the Flood boy, isn't it? Leaning against the mailbox there? Those Floods all have that same shifty look."

"Yes, it's Irv. They let him out on parole when his father burned his arm."

"My dad is against all these paroles they're always handing out to fellows in the pen and the reform schools. He claims that's why our crime rate is so high. They can't stay out of trouble. Stacy, I have to run across the street to Mack's garage."

"Want me to go with you?"

"I'll only be a minute. Mom wants an itemized bill for the parts and work he did on her car, and Mack said he'd have it ready. So you go on in Downey's and hold down the corner booth for us. I'll hurry."

Stacy started for the drugstore. She could feel Irv's eyes on her. He looked pretty grubby and, even without looking close, she saw a loose homemade bandage around his right thumb. She guessed, by the challenging look he gave her, that he was waiting to see if she would speak to him.

167

"Hello, Irv."

"Hey, Stacy, wait." He came toward her, the heavy soles of his shoes sounding so loud on the cement pavement that she involuntarily looked across the street to see if Bruce was within hearing distance. He had gone into Mack's office.

Irv said, "I just been waiting to see if someone I knew was going in there. Downey isn't what you'd say real fond of me. Not that he's big enough to throw me out, but he could make some dirty crack in front of customers. I'm the sensitive type." His raucous laugh was self-deriding.

"You want me to get you something? Did you cut your hand?" There were bloodstains on the bandage.

"Yeh, I cut my thumb when I was taking a broken light out of a car. Not deep, but I'll need a good-sized Band-Aid. I'm afoot, and there's not another drug this side of Broadway. Guess I'll have to invest in a whole box—"

She broke in hurriedly, "You want the one with all sizes? That's the kind we get. It's fifty-nine. I'll get it for you."

Because the Belford littles used so many band-aids, she knew exactly where to find them in the store. She picked up a box and called to Mrs. Downey at the fountain, "I'll be right back with the money."

Outside on the corner, she thrust the unwrapped purchase at Irv, and almost snatched the half-dollar and quarter out of his hand. He would have liked to talk, but she said, "I'll see you later this evening—I'll give you the change then," and scuttled back into the drugstore. Through its glass door, she looked across the street. Bruce was coming out of Mack's office.

She paid for the Band-Aids, and dropped down to the corner booth, her heart fluttering. It hadn't quieted when Bruce came in, and she looked to see what mood he was in. For just such things as her interchange with Irv Flood had she and Bruce bickered and snapped at each other—and parted in anger.

But he was smiling, and he stopped to pick out a certain brand of cough drops. "Catch!" he called, and tossed her the small, rattly box. He turned to the fountain for Cokes. All was well. He hadn't seen ˅ her helping Irv.

They sat in the same corner booth, tipped the bottles to their lips, spun them between palms, and pleated straws into miniature accordions. "Just the same as the old days," Bruce said.

Stacy smiled back. *No, not the same. The magic is gone. I know there can be no peace between us unless I pretend to be something I'm not. Unless I turn sneaky. It's being me that brings on the quarrels.*

They sat in a long silence. What did we talk about in those early, happy days when we sat here? I remember his telling me that poetry never made sense to him until he knew me. He said that when he read, "She walks in beauty," he could see me coming toward him across the grass at St. Jude's. And I told him that I always felt safe and protected and shut off from the world when I was with him. Now that's what is wrong. He wants to shut me off from Obie and Mr. K and Irv Flood. And I don't want to be shut off.

Bruce was saying, "What's this about a supper party at your house tonight?"

Another time the imp of perversity in Stacy would have delighted in saying, "We're gathering together the hungry of soul. I asked Mr. K. You think he's churlish, but he's just a lost musician. Then there's Pearl who's on the lookout for another man. And the Floods that we give a wide berth to sometimes, but not when they're in trouble."

She didn't want him to come to it. She knew such relief when he said, "Stacy, I don't see how I can make it," that she scarcely heard his further explanation. His mother was having a Great Books discussion in her home, and she might need him to chauffeur some of the participants back and forth.

"It's all right, Bruce—don't worry about it. It's what we call Mom's uplift party. Gumdrops!—I mustn't forget. We've asked in various and sunder."

"Sundry, Stacy."

She knew where to find the gumdrops too. She was paying for them when the TV program caught her attention. "Yipes, Bruce, that's the six-thirty newscast."

"We're on our way," he said.

As Bruce drove home, she said, "This time, don't let me off in front of our house. Remember, when we first started meeting after school, and we both felt guilty because you liked me better than Katie Rose? Remember how you used to stop on the street back of our house because we didn't want her to feel hurt?"

He nodded. "We'd get out and say good-by under the shedding willow tree."

"That's right. And when I'd sing, 'Is that willow tree still weeping there?' you'd say, 'Don't sing that. Don't you know our willow tree never weeps?' "

He got out with her on the corner a block west of Hubbell. In those earlier days, they had leaned on and on against the gray trunk of the tree, reluctant to part. The ground they stood on this windy October evening was covered with lacy yellow leaves. Others sifted down in wind-driven spurts. "The first time we ever stopped here it was snowing," Stacy mused.

Cully came running up the block to meet them. Bruce stiffened in his old way for the onslaught. Stacy caught the dog by his collar and quieted him. "He used to give us away by whimpering to get out when we'd stop here. But then when I'd go home after being with you, they knew anyway. I'd go in with what Katie Rose called my Bruce look."

"Yes, and I used to catch it from my folks for being so late getting home from school." But he looked at her uneasily, as though there was something he couldn't understand in her wistful reminiscences.

"You were the first boy that ever sent me roses," she said.

He caught her hands and held them tight against his chest. "I'll never forget the flower shop wanting to sell me red ones. And then I saw the kind I wanted—the sort of yellowish pink that you reminded me of."

"They were Killarney roses. Oh, Bruce—Bruce," her laugh was catchy and hoarse, "where did the roses go? Why did our weeping—willow—have—to weep?"

Tears were coursing down her cheeks and, in sudden alarm, he tightened his hold on her hands and tugged her closer. "Don't cry, Stacy, don't cry. It's all my fault. I'm jealous of you. Everyone is so crazy about you—and you reach out to everyone. I don't mean to hurt you."

She shook her head. "It isn't your fault. It isn't either of our faults. It makes you mad because I'm me. And I get furious because you're you. That's why—we can't go—on."

"What do you mean? You said you were glad I came for you. Didn't you mean that you weren't mad? That we could go on the way we were?"

"I didn't want you remembering my being so hateful and banging out of the car. And I didn't want to remember you that way. We do awful things to each other. And to ourselves. Maybe if we were older—I don't know. Maybe we're not big enough—I don't know that either." Her hoarse voice frayed out thinly, "Let me have one of my hands back, Bruce—so I can wipe my nose."

He freed one. She hadn't a handkerchief or paper tissue in her pocket, but she picked up a corner of the full, pleated shirt to dab at her eyes and nose. Bruce stopped her and took out his handkerchief and did a more thorough job. He was the only boy she knew who always had an immaculate white handkerchief.

He took her hand back and held them both pressed against his hard chest. He had to bend his head to hear her whisper, "It was so delightsome once. I can't bear to have it get drab and ugly."

Through her hands she could feel the slow beating of his heart and his slow, heavy breathing. He didn't answer. Perhaps he too was remembering the bickering, the quarrels, the vicious words, and all the glossing-over apologies, because when she said, "Let me go home, Bruce," he reluctantly but slowly relaxed his grip.

She pulled her hands free. She turned and ran toward Hubbell Street with Cully galumphing delightedly beside her. She was almost home when he called to her. She looked back, and saw him holding up the gray envelope in which the ribbons had come, and in which she had put the packets of gum drops.

They met halfway between the willow tree on one corner and the Belford picket gate on the other. "My loverly green ribbons," she breathed.

They both stood irresolute—each unwilling to turn his back to the other and walk off. And then Stacy did what seemed the most natural thing in the world. She moved closer and lifted her face for his kiss. "Good-by, Bruce," she croaked in her hoarse voice.

There had been teasing kisses, and hasty good-night pecks before. They had shied away from kisses in the same way they had from endearments. But in the windy dusk with the leaves swirling like a golden blizzard about them, he drew her close. His tender, regretful, *man* kiss was their first real one, and their last. "Stacy, Stacy, I'll always remember you."

She wanted to say, "It'll be a nice remembering for us both now," but she couldn't trust her lips, with the taste of salt tears on them, to say anything.

She had to do the walking away. She didn't look back. She went through the picket gate and closed it behind her, before she sensed his turning and walking slowly back to the car he had left on the corner.

❧19❧

From six-thirty on, Ben watched the clock at the Ragged Robin. It was a quarter to seven when he heard the final gasp of protest from Les's car as he stopped behind the drive-in. By the time he reached the counter, Ben's white jacket and cap were off, and his jacket was under his arm.

Les wanted nothing so much as to go into details about the game-saving touchdown in the game he had just come from, but Ben said from the doorway, "Mom's waiting for me to move the piano."

But his fidgety uneasiness had nothing to do with moving the piano. It had to do with Holly's talk of going out on the town after a dutiful appearance at Mother's supper. He was worried about what it would cost. And worried for fear Holly would twit him for being a cheapskate. Although his checking account had been whittled down by tuition, lab fees, and a dentist's bill for an impacted wisdom tooth, he wrote a check for fifteen. Bess put it in her cash drawer and gave him three five-dollar bills, along with the stock remark, "Don't blow it all in one place."

He stopped first at the House of Hollywood on the Boulevard for Holly's sandals which would make her birthday complete. He didn't know that the stately woman, with a smile no warmer than a dollar sign, who asked him, "Is there something for you, sir?" was Madame Simone herself.

"You have a pair of sandals here that Holly—"

Before he could fumble out her last name, the woman said with a wise look in her eyes, "Holly Ward. You want to pay for them and take them with you?"

She came back with a shoe box, lifted one sandal out of black tissue paper, and set it before him on the counter. "That's Leonardo's jade and jet." She glanced at the bill, and added, "The balance is fourteen, eighty-five."

He could only stare at her, and repeat, "Fourteen, eighty-five! But I thought—I mean, she said—"

"It's a seventeen-dollar item. Tax eighty-five cents. Holly paid three dollars on them when we put them in lay-away for her."

He looked at the single sandal sitting on the glass

counter top. Seventeen dollars for nothing but a sole, a high heel, and a beaded strap across the toes! But he took his three five-dollar bills out of his billfold and handed them to the woman. She brought him back fifteen cents, the box wrapped in striped black and silver paper, and a "Thank you. Come in again."

He could say to himself through his teeth as he pulled away from the House of Hollywood, "You've been took, buster. You really have been took. You're one of the ones that are born every minute." So why couldn't he laugh at himself? Why did he keep right on going to the address Holly had given him?

It was a three-story apartment house with a flimsy attempt at luxury. Narrow uncovered balconies attached to each apartment, a fading orange awning over the door. In the small vestibule, he glanced at the listing of the occupants, each with its orange button for a visitor to punch and announce his presence. He pressed 17. The metallic voice that answered was Holly's.

"It's Ben, Holly."

"Did you get the sandals?"

"Yes, I've got them here with me." He couldn't say: You misled me, of course, and I know it. You gave me to think that one night's tips would finish paying for them.

"I'll be down as soon as I'm dressed. I'll put them on down there."

"Snap it up, Holly, we're late now."

He watched through the glass door for ten minutes before he saw her coming down the hall in her bare feet. She was swinging a scarf, and she said, "I won't wear it unless I need to. I don't want to cover up the dress."

His first thought was that she looked more *un-dressed* than dressed, with her long hair hanging straight, and her arms and legs bare. The dress from Bangkok had a pattern of dragons—or would they be chimeras?—in vivid blues and greens, with gold and black accents. She had said it cost as much as if it had been flown over by private plane, and he wondered about that, because it had no more material than he could have wadded up in one hand.

"Wait till you see how the sandals look with this. They showed them together at Simone's." Greedily, she yanked out from the wrappings first one sandal and then the other. She slid her feet into them and stood up preeningly. "They even match the jade necklace, don't they? Now every place we go tonight, I'll knock people's eyes out. And that's the way I like it. Let's go-go-go."

She uttered no word of appreciation to him for bringing the sandals.

. . . He thought of Jeanie Kincaid. When the Belfords had cleaned out the closet under the stairs to make room for their downstairs half-a-bath, Ben had found, among other cast-offs, a pair of red earmuffs. Because Jeanie was prone to earaches, he had given them to her. "I know earmuffs practically went out with bustles, Jeanie, but I thought maybe—"

She hadn't let him finish, but cried out in delight, "Red fur earmuffs! Oh, Ben, I'll be forever grateful, my eustachian tubes will be forever grateful." She had worn them every place they went on cold, windy days; she had bragged about her red fur muffs, one for each ear, to everyone . . .

Ben had driven two blocks when Holly said, "It's a shame, Ben, to waste even part of Saturday night sitting around with family and friends. What would happen if we didn't show up? If we just kept going?"

His thoughts were like a double neon sign. One flicked on, "You've got just enough in the bank to cash another check at Downey's Drug." The other was, "The folks are counting on your being there."

And because, for all his nineteen years he had been responsible, he said, "This lasagna supper of Mother's—"

"Don't mind me, but I hate lasagna."

He went on doggedly, "Mom's got her heart set on all of us being there. She think's it'd be nice to play requests the way she goes at Guido's. One of the guests wants me to sing "Danny Boy.""

"Oh, I can hardly wait to hear you," she lisped. "That's such a sweet song. I'll just break down and cry."

He didn't answer. As he turned onto Hubbell, she gave an angry shrug. "You won't catch Guy Mowbry killing a whole evening with his loved ones." Her voice was not little-girl mocking, but carried a threat. "I'm as sure as anything that he'll be leaning on the button of number 17 most any time now."

He turned sick with disgust at himself. What ailed him that he couldn't say, "Okay. Just to be sure you don't miss him, I'll take you home right now." He said instead, as he stopped at the Belford house behind the car he recognized as Pearl's, "We must be the last ones here. There's Miguel's little wheelbarrow, and that high-off-the-ground job is Mr. K's."

He walked through the front door with Holly. The hall was deserted for the moment, though he could hear the party festivity in the big room which was both living and dining room, and out in the kitchen. A strange feeling assailed him. He felt like an outsider coming into a house that was familiar, but still not his own.

A girl was racing down the stairs, and his ex-patriate's eyes noted that the tawny and gold flowers in her dress brought out the same shades in her reddish hair. She was struggling with the zipper in her dress.

Holly had predicted that she would knock people's eyes out wherever she went in her Bangkok dress and sandals. She made a good start on Stacy, Ben saw, as he introduced them. Stacy's blue eyes widened, but she said like a little girl who has cautioned herself to be mannerly, "I'm glad you could come, Holly. This isn't my whisky voice. It's all that's left of my rah-rah one. I made a 'Happy Birthday, Holly' on a cake for you. Only I ran out of gumdrops—I should have bought more—and I had to leave the Y off of Holly." She suppressed a giggle with the palm of her hand.

Holly made no answer. She stood without moving or smiling. Stacy moved closer to the hall light and said, "Ben, finish zipping me. There's always that one spot you can't get reaching up or reaching down." She dropped her voice for his ears only, "I was so short of gumdrops. What was I thinking of not to get more?—because the O in Holly didn't come out good. And so, when I left off the Y, the Holl looked like Hell." She squelched her giggle again.

The old Ben would have laughed. The expatriate didn't. The old Ben vaguely noted, and was troubled by, what looked like a gay act Stacy was putting on. But the expatriate didn't ask, "What's bothering you, kid?"

Pearl was the next to greet Ben and his date. She was standing just inside the living-room door, and she boomed out, "I'm glad you aren't any later, Ben. I could smell that lasagna the minute I turned onto Hubbell. Been drooling ever since."

Ben was accustomed to seeing Pearl in the unembellished white uniform she wore in the bakery. Tonight, she wore a two-piece lavender knit with bead trim, which was stretched to the utmost. She was necklaced and earringed, and came to shake hands with Ben in high-heeled pumps that also looked a little tight.

He introduced Holly to her and wondered,

though vaguely because of the general hubbub, why Pearl said without warmth, "Holly, eh! I've never met you, but I've heard about you."

Wouldn't you think Holly would answer!

Mr. K's soft-voiced and old-world courtesy seemed all the more noticeable after Pearl's loud gustiness. He bowed from the waist to Holly and made a small oration to Ben about the privilege and blessing it was to break bread with the Belfords.

Mother was suddenly beside them. Ben's outsider eyes saw a pretty, sparkling woman with high color in her cheeks. He saw too the shock in her eyes when she took in Holly. It wasn't the bedazzling pattern in the dress, or the skimpiness of it which left such bare expanses of arms and legs. It wasn't even the long and lank black hair the wind had blown into disarray, which Holly hadn't even bothered to smooth. It was that emanation of contempt and boredom which slowed his mother's warm smile, and her, "How—nice—that you could come this evening."

Mother did what Ben had often longed to do. She reached out and pushed the hair back from Holly's right eye and said casually, "I used to do that with Katie Rose and Stacy when they were little. I always told them they'd get squinch-eyed looking through a curtain of hair."

She was holding a bottle, and she held it out to Ben with her young laugh. "You'll have to open it. Mr. K bought it—it's anisette to go with the food and the red candles and Miguel's handlebar mustache. He says it isn't exactly a pre-dinner drink—"

"It's sticky sweet," Holly commented. It was her first remark, and she followed it with a lower-toned one to Ben, "Hurry up and open it so the drinks and dinner won't take forever."

Ben took the bottle to the kitchen. It surprised him when he felt so *not* one of them, to have Miguel and Katie Rose include him as though he were. "We're getting the wine glasses," Miguel said, and Katie Rose lamented, "And no two alike."

Miguel was straining his lanky length to pluck them off a high shelf. His red plaid shirt was pulled completely out of his pants. His mustache, the same shade of brown and as desiccated as the ends of corn silk, had to be pressed back on his upper lip between each handing of stemmed glasses to Katie Rose.

She was washing and drying them at the sink. "There're nine of us," she told Ben. "Rita can't come. Everybody's here but Irv."

She held the tray of glasses, while Ben poured the colorless liquid. The dogs set up a barking even before the doorbell sounded. Katie Rose thrust the tray into Ben's hands. "That'll be Irv now. You take them in, and I'll go to the door."

❧ 20 ❧

In the living room, Ben passed the tray to Mother, Pearl, Holly, and Mr. K. Stacy reached for a glass and took a deep sniff of it. "Licorice. Mr. K says this is better'n cough syrup."

Mother was just saying, "You give the toast, Mr. K," when Katie Rose brought Irv into the room. There were greetings and handshakings with Irv saying, "Excuse the left. The thumb on my right is all plastered over with Band-Aids."

Pearl greeted him, "Hello there, Irv. Hardly knew you in your best bib and tucker."

Ben's spectator eyes took in every detail of Irv Flood's outfit. The white shirt looked as though he had hunted it up and washed and ironed it himself.

It was dingy white, poorly-ironed, and so short in the sleeves he couldn't button the cuffs. He had turned them back jauntily. He must have rushed off to the shopping center and bought the olive drab cotton slacks off a basement bargain rack. (Ben knew those bargain racks well.)

But it was Irv's shoes that made Ben's heart wince in silent sympathy. Shapeless, heavy-soled. And so obviously institution issue.

He shook Irv's uncut hand heartily. "Glad to see you, fellow. Take a glass off the tray. You too, Katie Rose."

She was saying, "Irv, I think you know everyone here, except Holly. Holly, may I present—"

"I know Holly," Irv interrupted, "and she knows me."

Holly turned her eyes toward him with a most uninterested expression. "Do I?" she asked coldly.

"I should hope to tell you. I'm Bigsy's brother. I guess you remember that blizzardy day last December when I took you your birthday cake. Bigsy got laid up with a smashed foot from his motorbike. But nothing would do the guy—you had to have your birthday cake."

For what seemed a long moment there was a stunned silence in the room. At least four people— Mother, Katie Rose, Stacy, and Ben, himself—were turning those words over in their minds, "that day last *December* when I took you your birthday cake."

At least four people besides Irv waited for Holly

185

to answer. She took a sip of her anisette; it could have been from nervousness, because everyone else was holding his glass, waiting for Mr. K to propose a toast.

Irv went on, "Godamighty, the snow was two feet deep, and here I was floundering through it with that big cake box. And worrying about all the fancy pink roses and Happy Birthday, Holly getting messed up."

Holly still played the disinterested role. "You may have brought a cake—I don't remember—but you're mistaken about its being a birthday cake."

Irv thrust out his chin and took a step closer. "Just who do you think you're kiddin'? I went up to Pearl's and got it because, like I say, Bigsy had to coddle his banged-up foot." He appealed to the guest who ran a bakery, "Pearl, you remember that cake with all the pink roses and stuff, don't you?"

"I certainly do. Bigsy told the baker and me that Holly had never had a birthday cake before, so we made it specially fancy. And Bigsy showed me the jade beads, and told us he got them out of lay-away at Simone's for her birthday. Those the ones you got on?"

Ben's fascinated eyes were on Holly. He had never seen her nonplussed before. He had never seen her when she wasn't on top and laughing at the one who wasn't. For once her insolence couldn't carry her through. For here was Stacy saying with a rueful giggle, "All my worrying about not having enough gumdrops to put the Y on Holly!"

And here was banty-rooster Irv leaving her no
out. "Now do you remember?" he insisted.

Ben said, "Never mind, Irv, never mind. I guess
there's no law against anybody having birthdays
whenever—" He couldn't finish the sentence. For
without warning he felt his stomach muscles contract
with mirth, and he threw back his head and
guffawed so heartily that the wine in his glass
sloshed over, and someone—Mother, he knew later
—took it from him.

Afterwards, he could never explain to himself
what it was that struck him as so ludicrous. Or why
he wasn't outraged at the realization that *he* had
been worked along with poor, ill-fated Bigsy Flood
and, of course, Guy Mowbry, and no telling how
many others.

He couldn't stop laughing. Because he was
ashamed of laughing at a guest, he hurried out in
the kitchen. But it was within easy hearing distance
of the living room, so he pushed out the back door
and stood on the step in the rollicking wind.

He couldn't analyze it. Perhaps seeing Holly out
of her Ragged Robin milieu and sensing the reac-
tions of others to her, had started to break the spell.
He didn't know. He didn't care. For to him, she was
now only a vain, sallow-faced girl, who thought she
was much smarter than she was.

He laughed out his rancor against her. He
laughed out the illogical power she had had over
him. He laughed away the torment and the doubts
about himself and his way of life.

At last he wiped the tears from his eyes and went back to the party. Less than ten minutes had passed since Irv had said, "Just who do you think you're kiddin'?" and his mother's turning to him when he came back into the living room. "Here, take your drink, Ben. We're waiting for you, so Mr. K can give his toast." But in that brief time, Ben had changed from the expatriate in his home to the old, reliable, protective Ben.

Mr. K was being his flowery best. "Let us drink to the charming and beautiful women in the room and to the happiness of all of us gathered under this hospitable roof. May each one find his heart's desire."

Ben glanced at Holly. She didn't drink the toast because she had evidently drunk her anisette without waiting for it. She didn't belong here. There was that word he used in chemistry—immiscible. It meant not capable of being mixed or mingled. Mr. K, for all his bitter regrets because his livelihood depended on his wielding a needle and thread instead of a violin bow, was honorable and fine. Pearl, with her bluster and romantic eye, was kind and loyal. Even Irv Flood, with his tough façade and the many chips on his round shoulders, was still trying to find a place for himself. *Holy Moses,* Ben thought, *I owe the fellow a lot.*

Because he was Ben again, he hurried out to the kitchen to see how things were. He took the spumone out of the freezer so it wouldn't be like cement when it came to slicing it.

Because he was Ben again, he could say when he went back to the living room, "Holly was telling me on the way over that she hates to waste a good Saturday night sitting around. She'd rather go out on the town. So as long as I'm dead broke, Holly, is it all right if I take you home so you won't miss Guy when he shows up?"

"It'll be perfect," she said airily.

Mother, the hospitable, offered, "Let me fix you a plate of supper to take with you, Holly."

Ben answered for her, "She doesn't like lasagna. Get your scarf, Holly, while I make a phone call."

In the hall, he swiftly dialed a familiar number. He heard the familiar voice answer, and drew a relieved breath. "Jeanie! I was scared you wouldn't be home. Do you hate me?"

The pause seemed long to him, before a catchy voice said, "That's the—silliest question I've heard in a—long time."

"If I come after you, can you come home with me right away? It's Mom's uplift party. Will it be all right with your folks on such short notice?"

Another pause, and this time she laughed throatily. "The folks are out to dinner. All I have to do is put away the peanut butter, shut off the TV, and find my shoes."

"The wind is turning colder, Jeanie."

"What's a cold wind to me? *I* have red fur earmuffs."

"You don't say." It was all he could do to keep from singing out, "I dream of Jeanie with the red earmuffs." He said, with a residue of laughter, " 'Then bundle up the eustachian tubes—I'm on my way."

❧ 21 ❧

The party was over. The guests had said their good-bys and departed. Ben had left to take Jeanie home.

Downstairs, only Mother, Stacy, Katie Rose, and Miguel moved through the quiet rooms picking up, cleaning up, and holding a relaxed and enjoyable post-mortem as they did.

Upstairs, the littles were long in settling down.

It was when the supper had reached the spumone and coffee stage that a great furor had erupted through the side door into the dining room. The stormy petrels and their booty had returned from Bannon. Matt and Brian struggled in with a glass container about the size and shape of a window box for flowers. It was half full of murky water and rocks and green foliage and, no doubt, aquatics from the creek near Grandda's.

Jill, acting as commandant, was yelling out to them to look out, not to spill the water and not to bump her in the stomach as she edged along at the side of it.

"The saints have mercy," Mother had breathed.

Ben was the first to his feet. "Miguel and I will carry it up to your room. But you three scoot ahead and clear off a place for it."

"I have to watch the frog so he won't jump out," Jill explained.

"I can hold him down," Irv Flood volunteered.

Grandda and Lennie Flood followed in a more sane fashion with the luggage. Lennie had evidently gone to sleep on the drive in, for he stood, blinking sleepy eyes in the light, but looking a little less unsure of a welcome than he usually did.

Grandda said to the Belfords and guests, "Don't worry too much about the aquarium. It's fair doubtful how long the minnows, crawdaddies, and frog will all live happily together."

Lennie had carried his catch in a bucket. "I only brought me back three minnows," he apologized. "But one looks a lot like it was related to a gold-fish."

Katie Rose said, "Lennie, here's Irv." The reticence of boys! Irv said, "Hi, kid, looks like you're growing out of your breeches," and Lennie said, "You look just the same."

Lennie was anxious to establish his minnows in their new home. He knew where he could find a gallon jar with a wide top he could use for a fish bowl. "Would it be all right if I go on home, Irv, because I'll have to wash up the big jar?"

Irv said he would go with him. But Katie Rose, remembering Rita's insisting to Grandda that Irv meant to start Lennie on a life of crime, detained him by saying, "Irv, go ahead and tell Grandda and Lennie about your plans."

Katie Rose had to fill in the details because Irv told it in his choppy way. Grandda said, "Now that's pretty fine, Lennie. I'll be coming in to hear you play in the police band."

Katie Rose had given Irv the wrapped blue T shirt Rita had left and also her message that she would be home Monday. "You tell Rita for me," he started, but Katie Rose interrupted, "I won't tell her a word. This time you can tell her yourself."

She had opened the door for him and Lennie and heard him ask, "Is Dad back from the hospital?"

"He will be any day now."

"How's Mom?"

"She's better. She's up and about," Irv said and, in a low aside to Katie Rose, "I told her to lay off the booze—I was bringing Lennie home tonight."

So the last guest to arrive was the first to leave. Katie Rose heard his heavy shoes clunking down the Belford front steps.

Grandda had made an addition to the party and to the singing. But even Mother's playing the piano and Grandda adding his strong tenor to Ben's could not drown out the uproar over their heads.

"Sounds like a team of horses," Pearl said.

"Sounds more like a Donnybrook," Grandda said and, at her mystified look, "That's an Irish fight—the kind that everyone is welcome to join."

There had been much running of water in the upstairs bath but not, as Katie Rose well knew, for baths. And much pelting up and down the stairs, the banging of the refrigerator door, as well as heated arguing between Matt and Jill, one at the foot of the stairs and the other at the head. It evidently concerned the diet for their new acquisitions for Brian came into the living room to say, "We can't find any bread except what's got butter on it."

"Garlic butter at that," Miguel had said.

"The fellow that told us what to feed our fish didn't say anything about garlic butter," Brian replied soberly.

And when it sounded as though furniture was not only being moved but might come through the ceiling, Ben shouted up the stairs, "What's going on up there?"

A frantic chorus answered, "The frog jumped out and we're hunting for him."

Jeanie had gone upstairs with Ben. The frog was located in an open drawer and restored to his rock in the aquarium.

But now all was quiet on the second floor. Now Katie Rose wiped the dishes Miguel washed, and

Stacy put them away. Mother came into the kitchen and backed up to Katie Rose for her to unfasten the hooks and eyes in the snug, stayed bodice of her dress.

Mother went on with the post-mortem, "Pearl has her hopes up."

Stacy was standing on a stool putting away the assorted wine glasses. She turned to ask, "Mr. K?"

"Oh no. I think she's given up on him." Mother snickered. "I think it was his kissing her hand that gave her false hopes in the first place. I shouldn't laugh. Pearl's second husband was such a slob and was always batting her around. No wonder she was won over by a little gentle courtesy. No, this is Irv Flood's parole officer. Irv was telling her what a good joe he is—"

"Sergeant Henry," Katie Rose filled in.

"Yes. And Pearl remembered that she had gone to school with him. So when Irv mentioned that Sergeant Henry's wife died about a year ago, Pearl decided it was time to renew their friendship."

"Ah, luv luv luv," Miguel murmured.

Mother post-mortemed on, "It did my heart good to see the way Irv ate. He was through three servings of lasagna before Mr. K got a good start."

"It did my heart good," Stacy said, "when Irv showed up Holly and her cozy birthday routine. Imagine that little hijacker having birthdays every jump in the road! Just as soon as I'm not so hoarse, I'll call her all the names she ought to be called."

"We'll save our breath, all of us," Mother said.

"What did my heart good was to hear Ben's belly laugh. I'm sure I'll get the poor-demented-mother look from you young ones when I say I have a feeling that Irv was Ben's guardian angel."

"Not from me, you won't," Miguel said. "A lot of people are angels unaware."

Angels unaware. Where had Katie Rose heard that before?

"What did my heart good," Miguel went on, "was the way Ben shoved the little birthday girl out of his life."

"And pulled Jeanie back in," Katie Rose added.

She went into the living room to see if any dishes had been overlooked. Stacy was at the sideboard. "I'm dividing the gumdrops with frosting on their bottoms." They both chuckled, remembering how swiftly they had stripped the cake of them between Holly's leaving and Jeanie's arrival. "Black ones for you, Katie Rose, green for me, and the rest for the littles. I'll feed these red ones to Miguel."

Sidewinder was begging for one, but Katie Rose shook her head. "Sorry, little beggar. You've already had a very un-poodle diet tonight." She went on gathering up napkins. "It didn't seem right for you not to have a date for the uplift party, Stacy."

"How you talk! I had my nice Mr. K."

"What about Bruce? I didn't have a chance to ask you when you came home. Are things okay between you now?"

"They're okayer than they've been for a long, long time."

Katie Rose looked at her searchingly. Her lumious Bruce look would have meant they had made up their latest fight, except for a certain—was it resignation or relief?

"You broke it off! But you said you were waiting for a sign."

"I got it."

"You did! What?"

"It wasn't a what. It was a who. Irv Flood. It happened on the corner outside Downey's Drug. I heard him coming toward me in those clodhopper shoes. He wanted me to buy him Band-Aids, because he didn't know how Downey would treat him. I was scared Bruce would see us talking together. And that's when the red light flashed. Stop, it said. No girl should have to be sneaky about who she talks to."

So Irv, all unaware, had been the sign Stacy had asked St. Jude for!

She carried out the empty ash trays and dropped them in Miguel's soapy water. He looked at her in exasperation. "I have a system about what goes in first, and what follows after what when I wash dishes. So don't go dropping things in. It brings out the beast in me."

She didn't answer. For suddenly she remembered. It was her lit teacher who had said when they were discussing *Pippa Passes,* "So you might say Pippa was an angel unaware, whose wings brushed others as she passed and changed their lives."

And suddenly she remembered too what had given her pause that day when she stood at her locker and turned the pages of her scrapbook. She was reading over the summary of *Pippa Passes*. And the nebulous idea that hadn't had time to lodge in her brain before Rita Flood interrupted was that an angel unaware needn't be so naïve and untroubled as the heroine in Browning's poem.

A boy is let out on parole. He was no innocent, joyful Pippa singing that God was in his heaven and all's right with the world. In fact, there were more things wrong than right in the parolee's world. But he had still been an angel unaware when it came to clumping his bungling way into their lives, touching and changing them.

Harriet Cass had enjoined her audience, "Don't ever say, 'I'm going to write a play about this or that.' Wait until a character or a situation clutches at you and begs, 'Write about me. Write about this.' "

Katie Rose was clutched. She went on wiping knives and forks without seeing them. She was seeing instead—only dimly as yet—the characters who were taking over her mental stage. She was hearing a jumble of voices.

Why had she ever thought a writer needed the seclusion of an ivory tower? The mind had a front and a back yard. Her front yard answered Stacy's, "Ben's an awful long time getting back from taking

Jeanie home—what do you suppose is keeping him?" with a "What do *you* suppose?"

She could drain the coffee percolator and call after her mother as she went up the stairs, "Mom, here's a last cup of coffee," and hear her mother say, "Thank you, lovey. I was so busy playing requests, I didn't drink mine at the party." And at the same time Katie Rose was hearing music. Not piano music which she had so recently heard, but a harmonica.

Stacy said her good-nights, but lingered in the hall doorway to say, "Now if I'm this hoarse in the morning, I won't be able to sing at nine-thirty Mass, so you tell Ben to skip *me*, Katie Rose. Tell him it would be very serious if I strained my throat."

"And—it's—snowing," Katie Rose muttered.

"It is?"

"No. No, I mean where I am. I mean, go on to bed, Stacy."

Katie Rose was alone in the kitchen with Miguel. The front part of her mind said, "Oh, let's just soak the lasagna pan." In the back yard there was the rhythmic clunk of work shoes. Like the beat of a drum, sometimes loud, sometimes faint.

She said in a far-off voice, "I'm working on a play. Only the play is working on me."

Miguel, son of a writer, ran his soapy sponge over the stove top and said in a quoting voice, "Every visitation of the Muse is disturbing."

"All the characters are taking refuge out of a snowstorm. Only I can't see where it is—"

"Let them decide."

The splash of water in the sink was the emptying of Miguel's dishwater. She heard him say, "No use putting that little dab of spumone back in the freezer. I'll just finish it off. Want some?"

She murmured an unintelligible, "No—thank you."

The successful Harriet Cass had said, "Your mind becomes the stage where the actors—happy, bitter, hilarious, driven—take over. You are helpless. You know then that you are only the instrument, that all you can do is hold your material to form. And when that time comes, you know you are a writer, for better or for worse."

Katie Rose's fingers felt the urge for a pencil. She dropped down at the table and found one on the window sill. The only thing available to write on was a folded piece of brown wrapping paper, but that didn't matter. She reached for it, carefully skirting the gondola-shaped saltcellar. She didn't want any spilled salt. There had been enough, and more, of the unexpected these past four days.

She spoke aloud to Miguel and to herself and to the, as yet, nameless and faceless characters who were demanding to be heard, "At first I thought it would be so wonderful to win a prize, but now that doesn't matter. I thought it would be so wonderful to be pointed out as the girl that had a play put on by the Civic Theater. But now all that matters is that *they* come alive and say what they have to say so I can put it on paper for them."

"Ah me, Petunia. I doubt if you'll get much sleep tonight."

She doubted it too. But that didn't matter either.

She smoothed out the brown paper. On it her fingers wrote the title of her play, *Angel in Heavy Shoes*, and waited for the characters to take on flesh and blood and voice.

ABOUT THE AUTHOR

Lenora Mattingly Weber was the author of more than twenty-two books for young readers, including the popular Beany Malone series. Beany Malone was the first of Mrs. Weber's heroines, but when she finally married the boy next door in *Something Borrowed, Something Blue,* Mrs. Weber introduced Katie Rose Belford and, later, Katie Rose's sister Stacy, the heroine of her final novels *Hello, My Love, Good-Bye* and *Sometimes a Stranger.*

Lenora Mattingly Weber was born in Missouri, but her family left the state when she was twelve to homestead on the Colorado plains. She went to high school in Denver and after graduation married and lived in Denver. Until her death, in January 1971, Mrs. Weber conducted a monthly column in *Extension Magazine* and wrote short stories for America's leading magazines: *The Saturday Evening Post, Ladies' Home Journal, Good Housekeeping,* and *McCall's,* in addition to her writing for young people.

All of Mrs. Weber's manuscripts and papers and copies of the first editions of each of her books were presented to the Denver Public Library in a ceremony in her honor in November 1969. They are now part of the Colorado Authors Collection in the Western History Department of the library.